BV TW ... 3. 11

D1138990

Yellow Town

Haunted by the murder of his wife and by his own experiences in the war, Earl Navarro had spent many years journeying restlessly – and often violently – across the west. However, he finally found a place in which to settle and in this quiet Colorado town he could while away his time drinking whiskey, gambling and chasing women.

But, with Earl's reputation following him like a shadow it's not long before his idyllic existence is blown apart in a volley of rifle bullets that drag him into a vicious range war. Killing, kidnapping and torture will test his courage and resilience to the limit.

By the same author

Vengeance at Tyburn Ridge

Yellow Town

Derek Rutherford

A Black Horse Western

ROBERT HALE · LONDON

ISBN-10: 0-7090-8003-4
ISBN-13: 978-0-7090-8003-9

Robert Hale Limited
Clerkenwell House
Clerkenwell Green
London EC1R 0HT

Typeset by
Derek Doyle & Associates, Shaw Heath.
Printed and bound in Great Britain by
Antony Rowe Limited, Wiltshire.

CHAPTER ONE

'Tell me again what he did,' Bud Laskie said.

He was standing at the window looking out at the south-west trail. It felt as if he'd done nothing for days but stand by that window watching the horizon. The smell of ash was still strong in the house and his eyes were red from the smoke and from lack of sleep.

'He killed four men,' his son John Laskie said, not even trying to keep the awe from his voice. 'Two who held up a stagecoach, and two more who came looking for him after-wards.'

'And they're treating him like a hero?'

'Yep.'

Bud turned around, his wooden leg scraping on the boards he'd carefully laid across the floor. 'He was on the stagecoach?'

John nodded. 'Yep. Apparently they'd held it up before. This time they picked on the wrong passenger.'

'And the ones who came after him?'

'A cousin and a brother.'

Bud pressed his thumb and fingers against his sore eyes. John had tried to tell him the story of Earl Navarro the previous day after returning from town with his mother,

5

but at the time Bud had been preoccupied with damping down the remains of his new outhouse and the one wall of the main house that had been set alight, and after that he'd been busy repairing the damage with what little timber he had lying around. There hadn't been time to listen to tales of gunslingers and bounty hunters. But this morning was different; watching a trail hour after hour gave a fellow plenty of listening time.

'And you think I should ask this man – this Earl Navarro – for help?' he said.

'What harm could it do?' Jeannie Laskie said. Bud looked over at his wife. She and John had probably discussed the notion all the way home the previous day.

Bud sighed and wished he was better at putting his feelings into words. A man's family needs protecting and a man needs to protect them. Both things were important, one to the family and one to the man. When you failed it left you feeling empty and hopeless. He wished he could explain to her how much it hurt when she and John and even Elizabeth who was outside with the horses right now all suggested he needed help from a stranger.

'It didn't do any good when I went to see Sheriff Garvey,' he said. 'I practically begged him to help us.'

'I think Garvey's a coward,' she said. 'Either that or the Colemans are paying him.'

'Nevertheless.'

'Earl Navarro's different,' John said.

'How do you know?'

John shrugged.

'You ever seen him?'

'No.'

'What harm can it do, Bud?' Jeannie said again. 'We

need to do *something*.'

'How long before your brother arrives?' Bud said.

Jeannie held out her hands palm upwards. 'I don't know. I don't think we can rely on Frank. I mean, I don't think we can rely on him getting here very soon.'

'So I go into town. I see this Earl Navarro. I ask him to help us.' Both John and Jeannie nodded. There was a glint of excitement in John's eyes. Another poke at Bud's wounded pride.

'And what if he wants paying?' Bud asked. 'You think the man's going to risk his life for nothing?'

'He's a good man, Dad,' John said.

'You've never met him, son. Never even seen him.'

'I *know* he'll help.'

'Look at you,' Jeannie said. 'You've not slept for two nights. You've not slept properly for two weeks. We can't go on like this, can we?'

Bud Laskie ran a hand through his hair. He turned and looked out of the window again. There was real glass in the window. Real glass in all of the windows, and boards on the floor. He was proud of what he – they – had achieved out here so far. The ground was starting to take shape. The rains had been kind to them and good crops were growing this year. Up until recently they'd had a goat and two cows, chickens and hens and enough produce already to be able to trade for other essentials in town. It had been hard. But they had expected nothing less. They had planned for hardness. What they hadn't planned for was Thomas Coleman.

Jeannie came and stood alongside him. She put a hand on his shoulder and followed his gaze out towards the mountains where dark clouds gathered over the snow-capped peaks.

7

'It's going to rain later,' Bud said. 'If I'm going in search of this Earl Navarro then best I go now.'

Earl Navarro was drunk, a nice drunk as was his way, but drunk nonetheless. He was sitting at a table towards the rear of Gillespie's saloon playing cards with George Clancy, Bob Forrest, and Sonny Roux, all three of whom had figured to take advantage of Earl's drunkenness to win back some of the money he had taken off them over the last month, and all three of whom were failing to do so. The pile of money in front of Earl kept growing no matter how much whiskey he put down.

'I don't know why you boys persist,' Gillespie said, bringing over another bottle for the gamblers and wiping the table next to them. 'The only time you win is when he wants you to win.'

Earl smiled. 'I'm on a lucky streak, is all. Anyway, at least they're drinking for free. I'm the one buying the rotgut you call whiskey.' His voice was slightly slurred. He winked at Gillespie and George Clancy scowled.

'Be cheaper to buy the darn saloon ourselves.'

'No one's forcing you to stay in the game,' Earl said, still smiling.

George Clancy scowled some more.

'Treat it like a school for poker,' Earl said. 'Pretend I'm the schoolmarm.'

'You're too old and too ugly to be a schoolmarm,' George Clancy said. 'Now quit talking and deal.'

Bud Laskie stopped the wagon outside the barber shop. On the plank-walk an old-timer smoked a long white pipe and slowly rocked back and forth on a chair. From the length of his beard it looked like he hadn't been inside the barbershop in years.

'Mr Laskie,' the old man said. 'And your beautiful daughter, too. Good day to you both.' He spoke without opening his mouth more than half an inch as if he had a lump of tobacco wedged down between his gum and lips.

Despite seeing him on numerous occasions Bud couldn't remember the old fellow's name. 'Hello, Mr—'

'Mr Gallagher,' Elizabeth said, leaning forward to look round her father. 'How are you?'

'I'm well, thank you, Miss Elizabeth. I believe I saw your mother and brother in town only yesterday. He's growing taller every time I see him.'

Elizabeth smiled. 'He's not as tall as me though.'

'Nor as pretty,' Gallagher said, then switched his eyes across to Bud Laskie. 'If you don't mind me saying so.'

'It's OK,' Bud said.

'Did they forget something, your wife and your son?'

'No, they didn't forget anything,' Bud said. 'This is different business.'

'Different business, eh?' Gallagher said. He took the pipe from his mouth, glanced in the bowl, pulled a face and then looked back up at Bud Laskie. 'I heard that you're having a little trouble out at the farm.'

Bud felt his face reddening. Did the whole town know of his problems with the Colemans?

'It'll soon be sorted,' he said.

Gallagher nodded. 'I hope so. Be a shame for all that hard work you've put in to go to waste.'

'It's not going to go to waste.'

'No need to get riled, Mr Laskie,' Gallagher said, slipping the pipe back into his mouth.

'You seem to know everything that happens in this town,' Bud said. 'I'm looking for a man by the name of Earl Navarro. You know where I might find him?'

Gallagher's lips smiled around the stem of the pipe. It looked to Bud like the man had predicted what Bud was going to ask him and was pleased to be proved correct.

'Earl Navarro.'

'Yes.'

'Earl Navarro.' Gallagher was nodding now, as if many pieces of a puzzle were falling into place in his mind.

'You know where we might find him?' Bud asked again.

'Just how bad is this trouble you're in, Mr Laskie?'

'It's nothing we can't handle.'

'So why are you searching for Mr Navarro?'

'That's my business.'

'I was only asking, Mr Laskie. A man like me, the only interest I got is other folks' interest.'

'Then you'll know where he might be found.'

Gallagher blew out a thin stream of smoke. 'In the saloon, I'd guess. Same as always.'

Gillespie pulled another bottle from the shelf and placed it on the counter in front of Earl. The game was over and Earl, slightly richer, had wandered over to the bar to talk to Gillespie and Annie, one of Gillespie's girls.

'This is a nice town,' Earl said, his voice no more slurred than it had been an hour earlier. It always amazed Gillespie how much the fellow could drink. It amazed him more that he never got violent or nasty with it the way most of the fellows did. Mind you, looking at George and Sonny and Bob over there, they were laughing too. It seemed that just being around Earl made a man see the good side of life. Of course, they'd all heard the stories – stories that Earl himself was always at pains to play down, though he never came right out and confirmed or denied them – about his life. What he couldn't deny was the scar on his cheek where, so the story went, a bullet had grazed him, and the scars on his hands that looked like knife marks. He'd lived a violent life for sure, but look at him now, he had his arm around Annie's waist and was whispering something to her. She laughed. Now Earl leaned back against the bar and started humming an old song, something from the war fifteen years previous. A song from the Confederacy. No one was bothered. Though it had to be said, Earl couldn't sing. Now another of Gillespie's girls was coming down the stairs at the back of the saloon.

'A drink for Francesca!' Earl called.

Francesca smiled, walked nicely across the room and thanked Earl with a kiss on the cheek.

Then the saloon doors swung open and a thin man silhouetted against the afternoon sun said, 'I'm looking for Earl Navarro. Is he here?'

Gillespie saw Earl's hand drop instinctively to a gun that he wasn't wearing.

For a moment Earl thought that some part of his past had caught up with him. As his fingers snatched at thin air and a voice inside his head scolded him for dropping his guard in this Colorado town miles from anywhere, his brain flashed backwards across the years throwing up images of dead robbers, hanged rustlers, weeping wives and blue-coated soldiers lying in pools of red. But all of that was far behind him now. And there was no one of this man's build whom he could place in this vicinity with a grudge against him.

'Who wants him?' Earl said, casually, almost impercep-tibly, pushing Francesca away to safety. The drunkenness had dropped away from him like a slicker being discarded when the sun broke through.

'My name is Bud Laskie. Is Earl Navarro here?'

'Haven't seen him in days,' Earl said. 'You got a message we can pass onto him if he ever comes back?'

Now the man stepped forward. Earl noticed he walked with a very slight awkwardness favouring his right side. He glanced at the man's feet. He was wearing a boot on his right foot but at the bottom of his left trouser leg there was just a stump of wood visible. Now Earl relaxed a little. He didn't know Bud Laskie, but he'd heard of him. Not that he'd taken much notice of stories about the farmer. It was just the fact of a one-legged man out there working a farm that had stayed in his mind.

'I've got it on good authority that he's here,' Bud said.

'Good authority, huh?'

The sunlight was no longer directly behind Laskie and it was easier to make out the man's face. He looked tired. There were lines of tension across his forehead, black shadows below his sunken eyes, and bones pushing up through his hungry cheeks.

'Is he here?' Bud asked again.

Earl Navarro stepped closer to the man. There was no danger here and he felt the alcoholic buzz returning to his veins.

'I'm Earl Navarro,' he said.

'You just said that he hadn't been seen for days.' The man's voice was as tired as his eyes and as tense as his fore-head.

'Ain't that a thing,' Earl said, and someone sniggered

across the room.

'I need your help,' Bud said.

'You're the farmer, ain't you? With just one leg.'

'I'm as good as any man,' Bud said.

'But you need my help?'

'Yes.'

'I don't know nothing anything about farming.' Another snigger.

'It's not about farming. I'm having some trouble with Thomas Coleman. The Double C ranch?'

'Not heard of it,' Earl lied.

'He tried to burn me out.'

'There's a lot of it about.'

'It's not funny, Mr Navarro.'

'I wasn't laughing, Mr Laskie. You tried talking to the sheriff?'

'Sheriff Garvey didn't care to help.'

'Really? Yet you want me to?'

'Yes.'

Earl shook his head. 'I'd say you ought to talk to Sheriff Garvey again, Mr Laskie. See, when it comes to law and order, he's got authority 'round here.'

'Either he's a coward, or he's in Coleman's pocket,' Bud said.

'You want to be careful calling a man a coward,' Earl said.

'I believe it to be true.'

'Well, anyway. I'm sorry but I can't help you.'

'You don't even know what it is I'm asking of you yet?'

Earl could hear the man's breathing getting faster and louder, the way a man's breathing did as he approached a gallows or a gunfight.

13

'Whatever it is I'm not interested. I'm retired.'

'Retired?'

'Yep.'

Bud shifted his weight briefly. 'I heard someone tried to rob a stage you were on. Two bandits. I heard that you shot them both and two more of their kin when they tried to track you down.'

'That I did, Mr Laskie.'

'It doesn't sound like retired to me.'

'Firstly, they brought it on themselves. Secondly, it was long ago and far away.'

'Long ago? Far away? I thought it was here?'

Earl shook his head. 'Some stories tend to follow a man round no matter how quick he runs.'

'I really need your help, Mr Navarro. I doubt you'll even have to do anything.'

'Just my mere presence will suffice, huh?'

'Maybe so.'

'What have you done to Mr Coleman to bring this problem on yourself?'

'I have water on my acreage that he wants.'

'Can you not share it?'

'I've offered. He didn't like the conditions.'

'Conditions, huh? I can understand that. Most men shy away from conditions.'

'I'm a farmer. I've worked hard on my fields. I won't have them trampled to waste by his herds.'

'And you want somebody to enforce your conditions?'

'Yes.'

'I'm sorry, Mr Laskie.'

Now Bud took a step forward. 'It wouldn't take much for a man like you to help a man like me,' he said.

14

Earl shook his head. 'I don't even know who's in the right.'

'I'm in the right!'

'I'm sorry.'

'Please!'

Now Earl noticed Bud's wagon for the first time. He looked over the man's shoulder, out above the swinging doors of Gillespie's saloon, and at the pretty young girl sitting upright there, holding the horse's reins patiently. He was getting tired of the conversation. He wanted some more drink. He wanted to get back to singing his songs and squeezing Annie's waist.

'I'll make a deal,' he said to Bud.

'Yes! Anything.'

'I'll help you in exchange for your daughter. That is your daughter, no?' He looked again at the girl outside. She sensed his gaze for she turned her head his way. His heart began to beat a little faster. She was very beautiful. But it wasn't that. The line of her mouth, the shape of her chin and of her eyes, from this distance she looked remarkably like Jessica. Jessica who had once been his wife.

'What?' There was anger as well as tension in Bud's voice now.

'Don't worry, I'm not talking marriage. Just . . . I don't know. Shall we say, two nights?'

Now there was laughter from the others in the bar-room.

'You can go to hell,' Bud said.

'So that's not a deal then?'

'I don't need your help,' Bud said, turning away. His limp more pronounced now as fury made him hurry. Then he turned again. 'This is a yellow town! You've got a yellow sheriff and you're just as bad, Navarro. You're not retired: you're a coward too!'

Bud Laskie didn't wait for an answer. He turned and was gone. A moment later they heard the crack of leather and Laskie's wagon pulled away.

'You going to let Peg Leg Laskie call you a coward?' Sonny Roux asked.

'He didn't mean it.'

'Sounded like he meant it to me.'

'I riled him.'

'You were funny, Earl,' Bob Forrest said.

'It must have taken a lot for that man to come into town and ask for help.'

'You thinking you made a mistake?' Annie asked.

Earl looked out of the door at the place where Laskie's wagon had been. He thought of Laskie's daughter and that in turn made him remember Jessica again. He wasn't in the mood for melancholy so he turned to Annie and smiled. 'No,' he said. 'I'm not aiming to get myself shot over a stranger's pool of water. Maybe I could have been kinder over the way I said no. But what the hell? Let's have another drink.'

It was two days later, almost to the hour, when Rufus Lee Chase who worked at the livery stable and sometimes tended bar in Gillespie's and who had even helped with Bud Laskie's harvest the previous summer burst into the saloon.

'Bud Laskie's dead,' he said. 'He's hanging from the tree down at Chapman's Junction.'

CHAPTER TWO

By the time Earl Navarro reached Chapman's Junction there was already quite a crowd gathered. He stopped on top of the rise to the east of the junction and looked down at the people milling about below. One man had scaled the cottonwood from which Bud Laskie's body hung and was sawing through the rope with a knife. Two more held onto Laskie's legs – real and artificial – as if to leave him fall when the rope was finally cut would be one humiliation too far. Other men stood around talking and watching. One was pointing along the trail that wound west from the junction. Earl hadn't paid a great deal of attention to these things in the month that he had been in town but he believed that the trail led to the Coleman ranch. In the far distance the great divide began to rise up from the plains. Snow-capped mountains speared the blue sky and looking at them filled Earl with both a chill and a longing. He'd known more than a few men go into those mountains and never come out. Below, a wagon pulled up. It had a tarpaulin on the back. The black-coated driver climbed down and walked to the rear of his wagon. He pulled the tarp aside revealing a coffin. Now Earl noticed Laskie's daughter down there. She was sitting on a grey horse a short distance from the crowd watching her father's body being lowered to the ground. As with the day he'd first seen her she must have sensed something for now she looked up at him. He couldn't make out her expression, but he could feel the hardness of her gaze and there was no mistaking when she leaned slightly to the right and spat on the ground before wheeling her horse away from him.

He turned his own horse and headed back to town.

In the first-floor room he rented at Louisa Glanton's boarding-house he retrieved his guns. He wore two, although he favoured the right. Colt Army model .44s converted to breech loading. Strapping the guns on now he realized how much he'd missed them, but the feeling brought confusion too. He'd grown to like the quiet life in this Colorado town where no one held a grudge over him and which was far enough away from his past that he could relax and cease looking over his shoulders every forty yards. He'd even found himself harbouring dreams that it might be here that he'd finally found somewhere to settle. He didn't know what he would do. Sooner or later he'd have to find a way of making a living but it hadn't been necessary yet. He'd built up quite a stake over the last few years and seemed to have the lucky touch with the cards. He was still where he'd started money wise, and that included board and food.

But as he buckled the gunbelt into place (needing to use an extra hole of length he noticed with some surprise) and tied the holsters down he felt like he was coming home. And in that moment he understood that for him home would never be a quiet town, a farm, or a perma-nent seat at a card game. For him home was the feeling of having well-used guns on his hips, and the willingness to keep on using them.

He rolled up a blanket and went downstairs. In the kitchen he told Louisa he'd be gone a few days. She saw the guns and her face whitened.

'It's nothing to worry about,' he told her.

'I'd heard stories that you'd given up that life,' she said. 'I'd hoped they were true.' Louisa was a pretty woman. Maybe forty years old. Earl had a sneaking suspicion that she would have liked him to have been more than just one of her boarders. He wasn't sure why this suspicion had grown in him. She'd never actually said anything or done anything to make him suspect this, but there were times when he caught her looking at him and there were times when she smiled at him in a way that he didn't believe she smiled at any of the other men who stayed there. Not that it meant anything. The other boarders were either old-timers whiling away their years crossing the road from Louisa's to Gillespie's and back again or they were itiner-ants who came and went and hardly left more than a dent in their mattresses and some spit on the floor.

'I guess there are some things that a man can't leave behind,' he said.

'Is this to do with the Laskies? I heard about what happened in the saloon the day before yesterday. I was proud of you, Earl.' Now she gave him one of those special smiles, although this one came with sadness in her eyes.

'Someone's killed Bud Laskie,' he said.

Her eyes widened. 'When?'

'I don't know. They found the body this morning.'

She put a hand over her mouth. 'His poor wife.'

'And daughter.'

'They've a son, too.' She shook her head. Earl wondered what she was thinking. She had the ways of a mother herself, but she used such ways on her boarders not on any children. Earl had never asked her – it wasn't his place to pry – but now he wondered why she had never married.

'Yes, I recall seeing him in town with a boy,' Earl said. 'I must confess I never paid much notice to the man.'

She glanced down at his guns again. 'You can't take on board the problems of everyone in this land.'

'Tell me,' he said, 'if a stranger turned up here looking for a bed and some food but he had no money, what would you do?'

She thought about this for a moment.

'If he was really desperate,' Earl added. 'If you could tell from his very demeanor that he was at the end of his rope, so-to-speak.'

'I'd probably take him in,' Louisa said. 'At least for one night. If I had room, that is.'

Earl smiled. 'I know you too well, Louisa. You'd have taken him in and fed him even if you had no room.'

She smiled back. 'Probably.'

'Definitely.'

'I think there's a big difference in giving a man some food and a place to sleep and going after his enemies with a gun,' she said.

He shook his head. 'I'm not so sure. We all have our own specialties. The man came to me for help and I turned him down.' Now Earl raised a fist to his mouth. He thought for a moment and then added, 'I didn't just turn him down: I poked some fun at him. I wasn't kind in my refusal.'

'Earl,' she said. She stepped towards him, then realized what she was doing, stopped, changed her mind and came to him anyway. She took his hands in her own. 'You're not a cruel man. I'm sure whatever you said it wasn't that awful.'

He liked the soft touch of her fingers on his own. It brought back those feelings he had harboured about a new life, a *different* life. 'I was drunk,' he said. 'Well, not *drunk* drunk. But drunk.'

'I've seen you drunk,' she said. 'You're not nasty; you're funny. I've seen nasty drunks and you're not one of them.'

'I doubt Bud Laskie thought I was funny.'

'So you feel guilty?'

He nodded.

'It still doesn't mean you did the wrong thing. You can't make the whole world all right.'

'I can try,' he said. Now, reluctantly, he let go of her fingers. 'At least I can try and make up for what I did.'

'You didn't do anything.'

'Exactly.'

When he got to the Laskie farm he saw two men digging a grave beneath one of the stunted trees on the higher ground that marked the eastern border of the Laskie acreage. The wagon with Laskie's coffin was down by the cabin that Laskie had built, first with sods of earth, then later with timber. There were several people milling around by the cabin door, others walking in and out.

Earl Navarro heeled his horse and rode down the trail towards a reception that was likely to be as unfriendly as any he'd ever endured.

It was the boy who saw him first. An older boy than Earl

had expected or remembered. Already tall, and as thin as his father had been, the boy had been sitting with his back up against the cabin, looking out at the trail and the mountains in the far distance, the sky clear and cloudless with just the black specks of distant hawks breaking the perfect blue. The boy's eyes were red and there were streaks down his cheeks where tears had fallen and washed away the dirt.

Earl braced himself for words that would cut deeper than a Cheyenne tomahawk. But the boy didn't recognize him.

'My pa's dead,' the boy said.

Earl nodded. 'I know. I'm sorry.'

'You don't look like the preacher. We're expecting the preacher.'

'I'm no preacher, I'm afraid.'

'I didn't think so. Can't imagine they'd let a preacher wear guns.'

'What's your name, son?'

'John Laskie.'

'My name's Earl, John Laskie. Earl Navarro.'

The boy's face changed in an instant. He reddened beneath the weather browned skin and suddenly he was crying again and screaming at Earl about how he was the coward that wouldn't help them and how it was Earl's fault that his pa was dead and how he was going to kill Earl and by God he better get down off that horse and fight like a man not like some yellow critter who just wanted to hide behind a bottle of whiskey.

Earl was aware that people were looking at him. The boy's cries had reached the grave-diggers who paused in their labours to stare down at the commotion. John

Laskie's mother and sister and several women from the town spilled out of the doorway. The cabin didn't look big enough to hold them all.

'Who are you?' John Laskie's mother said. Earl now recalled seeing the lady in town on a few occasions.

He didn't get chance to reply. John Laskie said something but the words were all mixed up in sobs. His sister's voice was clearer. 'That's Earl Navarro,' she said.

Jeannie Laskie looked at him. He could see the hurt and the pain, the hopelessness and now the fury in her eyes. She needed to let it all out and he knew he was to be the recipient.

But she simply said, 'Go. Turn around and go.'

'I came to say—'

'I don't want to hear anything you have to say. Please turn around and go.'

'He's a coward, Ma. He won't even get down and fight me!' John Laskie said.

'I know he's a coward, John. He's not worth your attentions.'

'I want to fight him, Ma.'

The daughter, Elizabeth, was staring at him with equally as much contempt as the others. He recalled her spitting on the ground when she'd seen him a few hours earlier. He sat motionless and let them hate him.

'Didn't you hear me?' Jeannie said. 'I asked you to go.' This time her voice cracked slightly.

'I came to say I'm sorry.'

'We don't want to hear anything you've got to say,' Elizabeth said.

'We don't need your sympathy,' Jeannie said.

'Nevertheless—'

'Nevertheless nothing!' Jeannie said, shouting now, tears springing from her eyes. 'Will you just go?'

'I was wrong not to help,' Earl said. He wondered if the daughter knew of his obscene offer to Bud Laskie.

'Just go!'

One of the men who had been in the crowd by the side of the cabin now came forward. He was dressed in a black coat and a black vest. A gold chain glinted from one pocket. Earl vaguely recognized him from town but couldn't name or place him.

'I think you should go, Mr Navarro,' the man said. 'It's clear that the family don't want you here.'

Earl looked at the man, then at the boy, his sister and his mother. Then he wheeled his horse around and left them to their funeral.

CHAPTER THREE

Thomas Coleman said, 'The man's been buried for two days now. I think it's time we helped his wife and kids make up their mind about leaving.'

He was a tall, wide-shouldered man with thick greying hair, bushy eyebrows and a beard to match. It was rare that he smiled and the lines of his moustache accented the almost permanent downturn of his mouth. His eyes, hooded by his brows, were dark and cold and often looked more black than brown. He wore expensive clothes, including a neck-tie, even when on horseback, and it was not uncommon for him to beat a man with a riding crop for simply being within hitting distance.

Coleman had owned vast herds of longhorns back in Texas. After a few false starts several successful drives to the Denver railhead had multiplied his fortune. Eventually he moved almost his entire operation into Colorado albeit with a steady feed of stock from Texas, slowly increasing his land holdings and driving out smaller operators. Things had now reached the point that he was rich enough to buy out anyone whose range, farm, or home-stead was in the way of this expansion.

Paying for such land was one thing, but it was always

more interesting when someone refused to take his money.

Bud Laskie was the latest in a series of such stubborn folk. Laskie had a nice parcel of land. Fertile virgin earth that he'd worked well for a year or two, low hills and a few hardy trees to the east – just enough to break up the worst of the wind – beneath which he'd built his home, and a creek running right along the middle. Water enough for irrigation and the few animals that he kept. Water right outside his door as near as damn. It was almost like having one of those fancy houses back East.

Thomas Coleman didn't need that water, but he didn't see that it would do any harm to have a little more. Besides, that wasn't the point. The point was he didn't want *any* landowner, water or no water, in the middle of his own range.

So he suggested to Laskie that maybe he ought to think about selling up.

Laskie had declined the opportunity.

Coleman had upped the offer. It was his final figure.

Laskie had pointed out that it wasn't about money. It was about a new way of life for him and his family. It was about staking his claim for part of America's new destiny.

Coleman had reasoned that Laskie could stake such a claim anywhere. Indeed, there were far more hospitable parts of the country.

Laskie had explained that they were doing well, thank you. Sure he'd heard of many people who had failed in similar undertakings, and he'd been told stories of locusts and droughts and tornados and all sorts. But the last few years hadn't borne out such pessimism. In fact, things were going fine. He got on well with the townsfolk – even

26

if they were extremely distant and even if he rarely saw them. They were kind and bought some produce now and again. He, in turn, employed some of them come harvest time. So, thanks for the offer, but no.

Coleman had flicked the riding crop against his own thigh and had quietly explained that this particular offer didn't carry the option of refusal.

'Are you threatening me, Mr Coleman?' Laskie had asked.

Coleman had smiled, warming to the idea of a confrontation but still giving the farmer one more chance. 'I'm simply suggesting you might consider my offer overnight.' Laskie was unaware of how rare such a smile was.

'The answer is no, Mr Coleman.'

'I'll come back tomorrow,' Coleman said. 'Talk it over with your pretty wife.'

'There's no need. The answer is no.'

'Very well,' Coleman said. And had come back that night with fire instead.

That first time they had burned down Laskie's original out-house. Another night they killed his goat and chickens. Coleman had come back a few days later and had said he'd heard Laskie was having a run of bad luck and wondered if he had changed his mind about selling up.

Laskie had run Coleman and two of his boys off the farm with an old shotgun and a mouthful of words that Coleman hadn't expected from such a God-fearing man. Coleman had laughed all the way back to his own ranch, his mouth aching with the smile that it wasn't used to.

Finally Coleman had decided to burn down the man's cabin – though the amount of work Laskie had put into it, it was almost a house these days. They set alight the outhouse that Laskie had rebuilt and then they set fire to the cabin. Riding away they thought they'd done the job, but somehow Laskie had woken in time to damp the flames down.

Several days later, two of Coleman's cowboys had run into Laskie a little way west of Chapman's Junction. They told Coleman later that the man had been red-eyed and almost delirious. It was either bad whiskey, no sleep, or a mixture of two. The farmer had attacked them. First of all unleashing his ancient shotgun on the men and then coming after them with a knife. He'd actually cut one of them pretty bad before they took his horse off him, shot him in his one good ankle, snapped his peg leg, and rode back to the Double C ranch.

Fearful of having the man found alive, or having him somehow crawl all the way back to town, Coleman and the boys headed back to where they'd left the man. They followed a trail of blood over a mile before they found Laskie at the junction itself, waiting and praying for a passerby.

Unluckily for Laskie it wasn't a busy trail, though it was only a few hours later that Rufus Lee Chase came by on his way to see Laskie himself about this year's harvest and found the man hanging from the only tree in sight.

Now one of Coleman's foremen, 'Moon' Barcelo, said to Thomas Coleman, 'What d'you want us to do this time? Try burning them out again?'

'I was thinking of running a herd over their fields down to the creek. I think if we ruin all their corn then that might be enough. But hell, the cattle are happy where they are and I doubt the Laskie woman is even thinking about corn right now, so yeah just burn them out. Do it right this time, though.'

'You want we should burn *them* too?' Barcelo said with no trace of emotion. If Coleman wanted Laskie's wife and kids burned alive then Barcelo would arrange it. If Coleman wanted them to get out, then that was fine too.

'Leave that one to the gods,' Coleman said, 'Just make sure you raze everything else to the ground.'

'No problem, boss.'

'And another thing.'

'What's that?'

'I want you to take Jared.'

'Jared?'

'Yes. Do you have a problem with that?'

'No, but. . . .'

'You think he's too young for such work?'

'He's your son, boss.'

'He's fourteen. He's old enough for such work now.'

Barcelo nodded. 'I'm sure he'll be fine.'

'I'm sure, too. It runs in the family.'

Earl Navarro heard them before he saw them.

For three nights he had been sitting, unbeknown to the Laskies, wrapped in his blanket in the darkness of a dry gully that cut across the sloping land behind the Laskie farm. Each morning he rose before dawn, prayed to no one and nothing in particular that things wouldn't happen in his absence, and then rode back to town to eat breakfast with Louisa, sleep for several hours, show his face in Gillespie's, then pick up some food for the coming night, before heading back to the farm. Louisa seemed happy that nothing was happening out there, but perturbed by the fact that Earl was longing for it to do so. She wondered aloud how long he was going to keep it up. 'As long as it takes,' he told her.

'What if nothing happens?'

'It will.'

Now the distant tremble of hoofs on the ground made Earl sit up, one hand on his Winchester rifle and one cupped behind his ear. The sound grew louder, carrying on the still night air. He sensed that there were three of them. He looked outwards at the darkness of the plain. The moon was a few days new and the sky was clear allowing starlight to illuminate the rocks and the gullies and the sagebrush laid out before him. He didn't look for anything in particular. Any of those shapes could be a man or even a horse in the strange imaginative moments of the early hours. Instead, he let his eyes rove, almost unfocused, over the black and grey landscape, the distant mountains serving as a dark background giving a little extra cover to the approaching riders. He was relying on movement to attract his attention, trusting, as he had done so many times, in his own senses not to fail him.

Then he saw them. A trio of riders indeed. Much further away than he'd thought. He'd spied them just in time for they stopped now and in doing so became just three more shapes out there in the darkness. But he knew which three shapes they were and he was able to follow them as they started moving again, slowly walking their horses forwards, the tremble of their hoofs no longer audible.

When they reached the fence that Bud Laskie had begun erecting around his homestead they stopped and two of them dismounted. They were no more than thirty yards from the house now, maybe sixty yards from where Earl was wrapped in his blanket.

He let the blanket fall from his shoulders, confident that the movement would not be seen with the darkness of the rise behind him and most of his body hidden within the gully, and raised the rifle.

Both men untied something from their horses and carried the items forward towards the Laskie cabin. One of the men stopped and knelt down. There was the flare of a lucifer being scraped into life. It went out. Earl heard the man curse quietly. Now it became apparent that they were torches that the men were carrying. On his second attempt the man successfully lit one of the torches. It illuminated his face in a series of grotesque jumping shadows and yellow light. The man lit his second torch from the first, then his partner came forward and held out his torches for fire.

The two of them now moved quickly, half walking half running towards the wooden cabin.

Earl waited and waited. He waited until the men were just ten yards away from the Laskie house. Watching them down the barrel of the Winchester he could see that they were both grinning. He wondered who they were. Not Thomas Coleman himself, that was for sure – they were too young. But the third man, still sitting back there on the perimeter of the Laskie's yard, he could have been Coleman. But there again, it was unlikely. Men like Coleman rarely did the dirty work themselves. Earl's finger tightened on the trigger. A sickness rose into his throat. It was never good to kill a man. Earl had killed many and every time it had felt like he was killing a little bit of himself in the process, no matter that they would have killed him had he not been quicker or braver or stronger than they. But this was different. These two had no idea of what was about to happen to them.

Earl sighted along the barrel of the rifle on the man nearest the house. The man leaned back, his arm extended ready to throw the first flaming torch onto the roof of the cabin.

Earl squeezed the trigger gently.

The rifle roared and jerked back against his shoulder.

The man flipped over backwards as if he'd been kicked in the chest by a horse. The burning torch landed harmlessly on the bare earth.

Without pause Earl turned his sights on the second man who had paused in mid-step. Now he dropped one of his torches, shouted something to his colleague, turned quickly and looked right at Earl without seeing him.

Earl shot him.

The third man was shouting in the darkness, wheeling his horse, crouching down, calling to his colleagues. Neither answered. The first man's clothes were on fire where he'd fallen on a burning torch. The second man was lying still in the yard. Earl lined up a shot on the horseman. He was further away than the first two had been and was lying as far over his horse as he could. Earl sent a shot towards him, without aiming. He could have shot the horse – all three horses – and then gone down there and finished the man off. But he wanted the man to go back to the Coleman ranch. He wanted this story to be told.

The rider shouted again, but this time it sounded like his heart wasn't in it. A moment later he dug his spurs into his horse and galloped away. Now Earl could hear someone screaming inside the house. He watched the rider racing away from the house. Then the door opened and he saw Mrs Laskie standing there.

'Get back in! Close the door,' Earl yelled.

She paused for a moment.

'They're still here!' he cried. He had to check the two men he'd shot. He didn't want one of them rising up and shooting any of the Laskies.

Mrs Laskie closed the door and Earl sat still for several minutes, listening, watching. The flames had died on the man burning in front of the house. Somewhere way off he believed he could still hear the sound of the third man racing through the darkness. The other two horses had milled around for a moment and had now decided to follow the retreating rider. Somewhere a coyote howled. Then there was nothing.

Eventually Earl stood up. He walked to the second man he'd shot. His bullet had taken the man in the chest. The man didn't look old enough to be burning people out of their homes. He had a cleanly shaven face, a face that probably didn't need to be shaved, the skin smooth and unlined. Earl felt the sickness rising inside him again. It was more difficult to ascertain the age of the first man. His hands and face were burned black.

They were both dead.

Now he knocked on Mrs Laskie's door. When she opened it she had an old Springfield rifle-musket in her hand and a mean look on her face. Behind her, Earl could see the youngsters. The boy looked both frightened and excited. The daughter appeared to be as angry as her mother.

'It's safe now, Mrs Laskie,' he said.

She looked past him towards the two bodies laid out in

the moonlight. For a moment the anger around her mouth softened, But when she looked back at him her lips had tightened again.

'What are you doing here?' she said.

'I believe it's a good job I was,' Earl said.

'We told you we didn't need your help. That we didn't *want* your help.'

'If I hadn't been here you'd have been inside a burning cabin right now.'

She didn't say anything to that, just stared at him. He didn't know if it was the coldness in her eyes or the venom in her voice but somehow she made him think of a rattlesnake. She could have had a pretty face too; it was clear where her daughter's looks had come from, but the good lines were made ugly by anger.

'You all might have burned to death in your cots,' Earl continued. 'At best you'd have been stood outside watching everything you own burn.' He paused, then added, 'You'd have been dead or homeless, Mrs Laskie.'

Still she didn't answer. He knew she wanted to be mad at him but also she would realize his words were the truth. 'It wouldn't have mattered,' she said eventually, her voice softer now. 'We're going anyway. We're just waiting for Frank to get here.'

'Who's Frank?'

'He's my brother. We wrote to him asking for help.' Now she looked Earl in the eye and said, 'On account of we couldn't get any help closer to home.'

He wanted to reply but there was nothing to be said.

'We don't want him to arrive to find us gone,' she said. 'But as soon as he's here we'll be going.'

'You're going to let them win?'

She shrugged. 'What more can we do?'

'You can fight for what's yours,' he said. 'You can do what your husband would have wanted you to do. You can avenge his death.'

'Mr Navarro, aren't you a bit late?'

Thomas Coleman was silent in his grief. At first he'd not been able to believe what Moon Barcelo was telling him. When the realization came that his foreman's words were true, he'd felt a pain in his heart as real as that in the palms of his hands where his balled fists were clenched so tightly that his fingernails ripped into his own flesh. He breathed deeply and blinked away unseen tears. The light from an oil-lamp flickered and danced in the corner of the room and the shadows moved over his face like living things. Outside, visible through the uncurtained window, the new moon looked like a cold silver coin being slipped into a dark pocket. He walked to a sideboard and poured himself a glass of whiskey and downed the contents in one swallow, then he repeated the whole act. Barcelo was telling him what had happened, how no one could have known that someone was up there, someone cold-blooded enough to shoot without warning.

'So you're saying it wasn't your fault?' Coleman said, the words hardly registering in his own weeping consciousness, Barcelo's answer not registering at all. Coleman carefully lit a cigar with trembling hands. He sucked on it greedily and let the smoke seep slowly from his lungs. He blinked several times more. He took more whiskey and felt it burning the raw nerves all the way down his throat and chest.

Barcelo stood before him, voice faltering, unsure

whether to say any more or not. He was ashamed and terri-
fied. He found it hard to hide either emotion. Riding
back, he had vomited in fear, not the fear of being taken
by a bullet coming out of the darkness, but fear of
Coleman. The man's fury was legendary and surely he'd
never had more to be furious about in his life than the
murder of his youngest son. Barcelo had almost lit out for
the mountains on the way home. At one point he'd even
turned his horse to the north-west. But that would be
admitting to a guilt that wasn't his to admit to. No one
could have foreseen what happened and he was determined not to run from it. And God knows he'd have been
running forever. Nevertheless, it had still taken more
courage than he'd realized he'd possessed to come back
here and face Coleman.

Finally Coleman spoke again. 'So you didn't even bring
my boy's body home?'

Barcelo swallowed. 'I would have been dead the
moment I tried.'

Coleman nodded, letting more cigar smoke seep from
his nose. 'You reckon?'

'I know.'

'You know, huh? Did you know that even the Lakota let
you bring your dead back.'

'Only after the battle.'

'You saying you left in the middle of the battle?'

'No. It wasn't like—'

Coleman raised a hand, silencing Barcelo. 'I know what
it was like, Moon. If you've never been shot at before—'

'I wasn't scared!'

'Most men would have been.'

'Well, I was a little scared but—'

'So you admit you were scared and that you left in the middle of the fight without even bringing my boy's body home? Papa Davey's body, too.'

'No. It wasn't like that.'

'So you keep telling me. I trusted you with my son, Moon.'

'It wasn't—'

'Shut up! I trusted you with my son and you got him killed and you didn't even bring his body home. You left him out there for the animals.'

'I couldn't have got any closer!'

'I don't think you should say any more, Moon.'

'But—'

'Quiet! Just go.'

'Go?'

'Get out of my sight. Get off my ranch.'

'What?'

Coleman turned away from Barcelo and looked out at the new moon and the stars up in the heavens. He was aware that Barcelo hadn't moved.

'Jesus, Barcelo, not only are you a coward but you're an idiot too. I must be mellowing. Ten years ago I'd have shot you by now. I never want to see you again. Every time I look at you I'll think of this moment and curse myself for not killing you. And one day I will. I'm going to turn around in a moment and you'd better be gone.'

Moon Barcelo went.

'What happens now?' Jeannie Laskie asked.

'We wait,' Earl said.

He was inside the cabin, standing by the window watching the plain for any movement. She'd made him hot coffee. His horse was tied behind the cabin with a supply of oats and water. It had taken a while but the hatred in Elizabeth and Johnny's expressions had softened and even Jeannie Laskie had accepted him and told him that though they hadn't wanted his help they were grateful to him. He admitted that he'd been a fool and had apologized for turning Bud away. That had raised a tear in the eye and a lump in the throats of the Luskies but at least they were all on the same side now.

Nothing moved outside.

Earlier Earl had picked up the bodies of the two men he had killed and had laid them on the Laskies flatbed wagon. He'd covered them in a tarpaulin and had then crossed himself even though he'd never really made up his mind about God. Moving the bodies around had brought back the nausea. He'd killed those men in cold blood. One of them had just been a boy. And this fact somehow brought forth images of Jessica. Images he'd never seen, only been told of and then imagined over and over, yet in the imagining the images were as real as if he'd been standing alongside her when the blacklegs had ridden into town and set fire to buildings and gunned down innocents – including Jessica, who was kneeling over a young boy they'd already shot. He could see her now, laid out in the dirt with her white dress drenched in blood and her hair blowing in the wind. And now he was as bad as those killers. He could have fired a warning shot over their heads. He could have even shot to wound rather than kill. He could have driven them away. Instead he'd done what he'd never done before and had shot men in cold blood. Why had he done it? Was it embarrassment at the way he had turned down Laskie's plea for help? Was he a murderer because fate had seen fit to make him drunk when the one legged farmer had asked for Earl's assistance? Or was it more than that? Was he still seeking revenge on Jessica's killers, slaying the bad guys one by one until maybe a day would come when the feeling in his heart would tell him that the scales had been balanced?

'For what do we wait?' Jeannie Laskie said now.

'I don't know. They might try something else.'

'Do you think?'

'I doubt if they'll try anything tonight, but I'm not going to leave you alone.'

'Thank you.'

He looked across the dark plain again. 'What would you do if you were them?' he asked.

She thought about it for a moment. A look of sadness flitted across her face. 'I'd want the bodies back. But then I'm a mother.'

'They've got mothers too,' Earl said.

'Just one man?' Thomas Coleman's eldest son, Lewis, asked.

'Moon didn't stick around long enough to find out,' Thomas Coleman said. 'But his best guess was one man.'

'Any idea who?'

'I've sent a couple of the boys into town to make a few discreet enquiries. I can't think of anyone who it might be.'

'I thought they were all yellow in town,' Wesley, the middle son, said.

'Whoever it was shot Jared without warning *and* from a hiding place. Sounds pretty yellow to me.'

'And if he's still at the Laskie place when we get there

you want us to kill him?' Lewis asked.

Thomas Coleman ran his hands over his tired face. 'I want him dead. But I want him dead slowly.'

Both sons nodded. Everybody had loved young Jared. Anyone who could shoot such a boy in the back deserved to die slowly.

'You want us to bring the man in then,' Lewis said. It was more an assumption than a question.

'I want Jared brought home. And Papa Davey. You do that for me. Take as many men as you need. If the opportunity arises then bring the killer to me. But don't take any risks. I'll have him very soon. I swear on Jared's grave I'll have my revenge.'

CHAPTER FOUR

The men came mid-morning. Earl Navarro saw them from a distance and quietly let himself out of the cabin. The Laskies had been awake most of the night after the shooting and it was only at dawn that they'd fallen into disturbed sleep. He loosened both guns in their holsters, cradled his rifle in his hand, and watched the approaching riders. When they were in range he worked the action on the Winchester, the sound clear and unmistakable in the still air. They slowed now. The lead rider pulled his own rifle from a scabbard. Earl raised his gun to his shoulder.

'Stop right there,' he said.

The men kept coming.

'I'm not fooling,' Earl said.

Now they stopped, maybe thirty or forty yards away. Too far for Earl to be worried about revolvers, but if they all had rifles and all decided to use them simultaneously it would be a close thing.

'You the one who shot our brother?' the lead rider asked. 'Shot him in the back?'

'If he was one of the two about to set fire to an innocent family's cabin then yes, I'm the one that shot him.'

'How come you never shot us?' another of the riders

asked. 'You could have hid up and shot us in the back, too.'

'If you've come to burn down the cabin then I will shoot you.'

The men looked at each other and laughed. One of them spat tobacco juice onto the ground. 'All four of us, huh?'

'All four of you,' Earl said. He wasn't sure that he'd be able to get all four before they got him. It depended on how they chose to play it. But he had no hand anyway. It was all bluffing.

'Who are you?' the lead rider asked.

'Just a friend of the family,' Earl said. As he spoke he heard a sound behind him. It was the sound of a door opening and a shotgun being snapped into readiness. He daren't look round. He was already at a disadvantage but it was a slight enough disadvantage that the riders didn't seem inclined to call him on it. To take his eyes off them might be the only edge they'd need. So he kept his eyes on the four riders and found himself praying again, this time that it was one of the Laskies behind him and not one of Coleman's men who had outflanked him. He felt a trickle of sweat run down his spine.

'And who are you?' Earl asked.

'Already told you, we're brothers of the boy you killed.'

'Was it your father who sent him?' Earl said, guessing that if there were this many kinfolk around then it stood to reason that a father, maybe Coleman, was in the background. 'Had his boy go off to commit arson.'

'Don't change the fact that you shot the boy in cold blood.'

Earl swallowed. The very same thought had been torturing him all night and all morning.

'We should kill you here and now,' another of the riders said.

'You can try,' Earl said. The rider's words suggested that they weren't here to kill him. Nevertheless he didn't release any pressure on the rifle trigger.

'You'll wait,' the lead rider said.

'You've come for the bodies?' Earl said.

'Yeah. You going to lower that rifle and let us come and get them?'

'They're on the wagon by the gate. Under the tarp. Help yourself.'

'The rifle?'

'It stays raised.'

'You shot our brother in the back; why should we trust you?'

'If I wanted to kill you I'd have done so already.'

'Maybe you should've done,' the lead rider said, walking his horse forward. 'Next time we meet you'll wish you had.'

'We'll see.'

After the riders had tied the two bodies to their horses and departed, Earl breathed out a long sigh of relief. He'd expected something this morning, something involving retaliation and violence. In a way what had happened was more unsettling than violence, not because of the threats made, but because so many of the words had been true. As he watched the riders slowly retreating across the plain in a cloud of dust he heard footsteps behind him. He turned and Jeannie Laskie was there with the shotgun in her arms.

'I thought we were all about to die,' she said.

'They'd have needed more than four men,' Earl said.

'So you told them.'

'You don't believe me?'

'Do you believe yourself?'

'It would have been close,' Earl said. 'You had a gun too, so we'd have been all right. Thank you, by the way.'

Earl smiled, but Jeannie Laskie didn't. Instead she said, 'Did you really shoot the boy in the back?'

In town, Old Man Gallagher rocked back on his chair until the rear of his head rested against the barbershop wall, took a draw on his pipe, looked puzzled until he realized that the tobacco was no longer burning, and said to Louisa Glanton, 'Some men was asking after you earlier.'

'Some men? What men?'

'Turns out they're a couple of Double C men. Coleman's men.'

Louisa felt a chill run up her back.

'Why were they asking after me?'

'So far as I can figure they were asking around to see who was out at the Laskie place. I think someone let it slip that it was Earl before they realized who it was doing the asking. I guess they asked where they'd normally be able to find Earl and someone mentioned you.'

She put down the basket she was carrying. It had suddenly become very heavy. 'What's happening out there? Have you heard anything?'

'Nope. Nothing.'

'I ought to go out there.'

'Earl can handle himself OK, Miss Glanton. Anyway, a couple of the boys have taken a ride out there this morning. We'll soon know if there's anything up.'

'What is it with Thomas Coleman?' Louisa said, her

gaze drifting away from Gallagher and along the two rows of buildings that lined Main Street. Where the buildings ended the mountains and the plains leading towards them could be seen clearly. 'Why is he so determined to have that land.'

'He doesn't need it, that's for sure,' Gallagher said. 'I suspect that as soon as he's got it he'll forget all about it.'

'He hates people standing up to him?' she said.

'More than anything,' Gallagher said. 'More than anything.'

'You have to leave,' Earl said to Jeannie Laskie.

'I've already told you, we're just waiting for Frank.'

'No. You've got to leave now.'

She looked at him and he tried to read her thoughts. What did she really think about this man who had at first refused to help her and had then come onto her land, killed two men in cold blood and, as a result of that, was now telling her she had to leave.

'I'm sorry,' he added.

'For what?' she said. They were standing outside, just the two of them. She was now looking out to the west, across the plains, maybe to the mountains, maybe towards Coleman's ranch that lay somewhere out there beyond view.

'I don't seem to be doing a very good job of helping you,' Earl said.

'They dealt the cards,' she said, using language that Earl had used the night before when they'd all been awake after the shooting.

'I'm not sure I've played my hand well.'

'Could you have played it any different?'

45

He shrugged. 'I don't know. I think the boy I killed was Coleman's son.'

'I heard,' she said.

'They're going to come back,' he said. 'They're going to come back with a lot more men: they're going to come back for me.'

'Are you scared?'

'I can look after myself. But I can't do that *and* protect all of you.'

'We have nowhere to go.'

'Go into town. Ask for Louisa Glanton. She'll sort you out with a room. You can use my room.'

'And then what? This is our home.' Together they turned and looked at the cabin, at the half built fence, and the wagon and the few animals, at the fields beyond, at John and Elizabeth talking together by the horses. Earl's eyes were drawn to the trees up on the rise where a cross could clearly be seen in the ground.

'When everything's over this will all still be here. If you want it.'

When he looked at her there were tears in her eyes. She had the tough wind-burned skin of a farmer's wife, but the sadness could cut through as easily here as it did in any Eastern lady's delicate world.

'I don't know,' she said. 'Everything's changed.' Then she blinked hard once or twice and said, 'What about you?'

'Me?'

'Yes. What are you going to do?'

'I'm going to have a ride out there and try and get a feel for the size of Coleman's operation. See what I'm up against.'

'And then what?'

'I don't know. Play my hand the best I can.'

'And if you've been dealt no cards?'

'Then I guess I'll bluff.'

'You can't take them all on.'

'I don't need to take them all on. Just Coleman.'

'And his sons.'

'True.'

'You're not the running type, are you?'

He smiled. 'I've been in worse situations.'

'We don't even know you,' she said. 'And here you are risking everything for us.'

'Once upon a time such work was my job,' he said. 'Now I realize it's all I can do. Anyway, less of this talk. I need you to leave. Will you do that? I promise you can come back afterwards, if you want.'

She reached out and took his hand. 'Be careful, Earl Navarro.' Then she turned to her children and told them they were leaving.

Coleman's ranch nestled in the foothills of the Divide, on a huge flat area surrounded by gentle rises. The ranch house itself was as big a building as Earl had seen west of the Mississippi. It was constructed of finely finished timber with brick chimneys and tiles on the roof. There was a high porch running all the way around the building with steps on each side leading up to large fancy doors. It was built in the lee of the largest of the rises and there were young trees planted on the exposed sides. A fine-looking outhouse was linked to the main building by a covered walkway, and a log fence had been constructed leading away from the house, although the fence stopped before actually encircling anything. Further afield there were numerous other buildings, though none near so fine as the main house. Beyond these he could see two corrals, one holding a dozen or so horses and the other empty. There were piles of manure and piles of wood. At the back of one of the buildings were several huge spools of barbed wire. There were wagons and buggies, horses and dogs and chicken milling around: it was like a small town.

And on the far side of the ranch in a small area where young trees grew and a low fence marked a perimeter a crowd of cowboys was standing around two new graves.

It was the second uninvited funeral he had been to in less than a week. And, in a way, he was the cause of both.

Earl lay on his belly and memorized the scene. For a few moments he was transported back in time to the days more than fifteen years before when he'd been a scout for the Confederacy. One of the best scouts, he liked to think. During the war, fellow scouts had been caught and shot and others had been captured and had begged to be shot. He'd been close enough to hear their agonies. Yet he didn't believe that a single Union soldier had ever known of his presence. Excepting those whom he'd killed, of course.

Using the telescope that he still retained from those days, and being careful to avoid the sun glinting off the lens, he counted the men around the graves. Twenty-two of them. It was all he needed to know for now. He slipped the telescope inside his shirt and then slid backwards over the slight rise he'd been lying on.

He was still on his belly when he saw the two cowboys waiting for him, guns levelled and the glint of victory in their eyes.

*

Jeannie Laskie looked up at the sky. 'It must be two hours since he went.'

The two men before her hadn't dismounted. They sat high on their horses looking down, hats shielding their eyes and faces, listening to her tell of what had happened the previous night and that morning. Jeannie knew these two men from town, Bob Forrest and George Clancy. She wasn't quite sure what they did for a living but she'd seen them around plenty of times, yet she was still careful what she said, not mentioning any of the circumstances around the shootings.

'I think we'd better head on out there,' George said. 'Just to check he's OK.'

'What about you, ma'am?' Bob said. 'You look like you're leaving. Are you all right?'

'Earl said it would be for the best. Especially now.'

'He said we can come back,' John Laskie said, from along-side his mother. 'We ain't giving up just 'cos of Coleman.'

'Good on you, son,' George said.

'You got somewhere to go?' Bob asked.

Jeannie Laskie nodded. 'I've got a name at least; Louisa Glanton.'

Bob Forrest nodded. 'She's a sweetheart. She'll look after you.'

'We'd best be on our way,' George said.

'Go carefully,' Jeannie said.

Then both men tipped their hats, wheeled their horses, and were away, the silhouettes of revolvers at their hips and rifles in their scabbards.

*

Sometimes Earl Navarro believed that killing came too easy to him. It had started in the war and had carried on ever since. He knew other men, some at least, didn't have it in them. He'd seen them tremble and shake so much that they weren't able to put a bullet within twenty feet of their intended target. Some were physically sick, not with cowardice – though the thought that they might be about to die was no doubt a factor – but with the enormity of the act. Luckily for them they usually failed to kill anyone and thus given time were able to overcome their sickness. For him it had never been like that. He killed with gun, knife, and rope and had never suffered outwardly with trembles or sickness. Until recently it had been a question of kill or be killed and thus he'd never hesitated, and it was this willingness to carry through on such an act that he believed had kept him alive so long. All the others had hesitated and he'd killed them.

He drew now, not thinking about anything beyond the split second ahead of him. One of the cowboys was starting to say something – 'Looks like we got ourselves a spy' – and turning to grin at his companion when Earl's bullet took him in the heart. The man's words became a liquid gurgle, his eyes widened in surprise and, as the second cowboy opened his mouth to curse, a bullet took him in the chest too, knocking him backwards, a crimson mist following him down.

The gunshots echoed out across the plain and, Earl knew, over the ranch below him. He sprinted across to where he had hobbled his horse and quickly turned to the east, spurring the horse on, only now feeling the shaking and the sickness rise over him.

*

50

Bob Forrest saw the galloping rider first.

'There he is,' he said. 'Looks like the Devil's on his tail.'

George Clancy watched Earl for a few seconds, the distant rider was coming straight towards them. He had a revolver in his hand but, as the riders closed together, Earl holstered the gun and reined up his horse.

'Boys,' he said.

'You're riding like there's a posse on your tail,' George said.

'That just might be the truth,' Earl said. He cast a look back over his shoulder. 'I figure I'm maybe ten minutes ahead of them at best.'

'Who?' Bob asked.

'Now's not the time,' Earl said. 'I'd tell you as we ride, but my advice is to stay away from me.'

'You're why we're out here,' Bob said.

'Some folks were asking after you in town.' George said. 'We thought we'd ride out to the Laskie place and check everything was OK. Mrs Laskie told us what happened.'

They turned their horses now and started riding east again. Earl pressed his heels into his horse's flanks and set a rapid pace. It was hard to talk at this speed with the jarring of the ride breaking up their words, and dust drying their throats.

'Have they left yet?' Earl said.

'More or less,' George said.

'I imagine they'll have set off by now,' Bob added.

'I don't want to take this trouble to town.'

'They brought it on themselves, trying to burn the Laskies out like that,' Bob said.

'Yeah,' Earl said.

'There's more isn't there?' George asked.

Earl nodded, but the movement was swallowed up by the greater movement of staying on the racing horse.

'What happened?'

'I killed two more.'

Bob and George looked at one another. Bob glanced behind them. There was no sign of anyone following, just their own dust hanging in the air. Now he looked at Earl, the man who had arrived just a month ago, full of smiles and good humour and denials of any of the stories that followed him into town, the man who had won all of their money and had somehow left them feeling warm and well disposed to him even as he pocketed their dollars. The man had a solemn look on his face now, even a paleness to his stubbled face that had never been there before. He looked troubled, Bob thought. And then he looked behind again and still there was no one there. Their pace was slowing now, either through tacit understanding or fatigue on the part of Earl's horse which was foaming at the mouth. Bob saw George staring at Earl, too, and he knew right then that there was no posse chasing them. The man had killed four men in less than twenty-four hours.

Who'd want to chase a fellow like that?

CHAPTER FIVE

Thomas Coleman said, 'The man is a murderer.' He looked at his remaining sons. 'A cold-blooded murderer.'

'Then why don't we go after him?' Wesley asked.

'We are going after him,' Thomas said. 'Just not in the way he expects.'

'I don't understand.'

'You will,' Coleman said.

When they'd heard the shots earlier, literally as the first sprinklings of dirt were being dropped down onto Jared's and Papa Davey's coffins, there'd been a few moments of panic with everyone running and diving for cover. One of the men – Cooky – had even dropped down into Papa Davey's grave though later he was absolutely insistent he'd slipped. When the panic had subsided and they realized that whoever it had been – and already in everyone's mind there was only one suspect – appeared to have gone, there were several minutes of chaos as cowboys grabbed horses and rode for the perimeter.

A few minutes later they'd found the bodies.

A posse was almost fully formed and ready to go before Thomas Coleman managed to calm them down. God knew that was hard enough to do. Inside he had been raging. He'd had a mind to take the lead horse himself. He'd done it before. It wouldn't have been the first time he'd strung a man up. But he'd not become the man he was without being able to control his emotions and his temperament. Oh they could ride Navarro down and kill him, of that Coleman had no doubt. But at what cost? The man was trigger-happy but he was also good. Four men, including one son, was already too high a price.

Anyway, in order to balance that death it needed something more than a quick bullet or a jerking rope. Something far more. Something akin to what the Indians would do in such circumstances.

So he'd broken up the posse amidst much anger and jeering. He'd told the boys they would get what they wanted. It had taken some doing but eventually they'd calmed down and believed him. After all, hadn't he always delivered on his promises?

And this time he promised he'd bring them Navarro alive.

Alive, and ready to scream.

'When I was in the army,' Earl said, 'I saw a fight. I'd only been in a few weeks. There was a little fellow who, on account of his size, we called Bean. Well, we never called it to his face because he didn't like the name and he had a vicious temper. But if ever we were talking about him we'd say "Bean did this" or "Bean said that". Anyway, the guy he fought was about twice his size. I mean, not just in height. John Dockery was as wide across the shoulders as Bean was tall. He could've swatted Bean like a fly. And he did. Bean came at him again and again and each time John knocked him into next week. It seemed like the fight was going to go on and on so a couple of guys tried to stop Bean, tried to tell him that it was OK, that he had nothing left to prove. But Bean shrugged them off and went after John once more. And got knocked down again. Except this time he came up with a knife in his hand. Right then John Dockery said enough was enough. He even said, "OK, you won this fight, Bean. You beat me". We were all on the same side. There was no point in killing each other. The Yankees would do plenty of that for us very soon. But Bean wasn't having any of it. He stood there with his nose flat and blood pouring from his mouth and he screamed at John to come and fight like a man. I guess John figured he could knock Bean down, take the knife off him, maybe hold it against his neck or something and *then* the fight would be over, because he turned round and took a step towards Bean, a kind of resigned look on his face as if the whole thing was becoming boring. And right then, right when John was sighing and cracking his knuckles and thinking about going for some coffee or something, Bean jumped forwards, feinted to the left and moved to the right and quicker than any of us could have guessed he ran that knife right across John Dockery's throat.'

Earl paused, sipped from the tin cup of coffee that was on the table in front of him, and looked out of the window at the south-west trail.

George Clancy sat opposite him smoking a cigarette. Bob Forrest was sitting on the cot in the corner also smoking.

'What happened then?' he asked.

'They shot him,' Earl said.

'Bean?'

'Yep.'

'And John Dockery?'

'John? He kind of stood there for a few moments with a look of surprise on his face, then he opened his mouth to say something and when nothing but blood came out he fell down dead.'

'Lordy,' Bob said.

'They'd have both been good soldiers,' Earl said.

'You're telling us this for a reason,' George said.

Earl nodded. Nothing was happening out there on the trail. There was no posse coming. Not in the daylight hours anyway.

'I'd never killed anyone at that point,' he said. 'I was sick afterwards. I couldn't imagine ever doing something like that. But war changes a man – a boy – quicker than you think.

'The first time I went into battle I recalled what Bean had done. I remembered how he'd taken a beating and still come out on top. I remembered how he'd never given up. I remembered how fast he'd been. And I learned very quickly that in war there aren't any rules. If you want to live then you'd better be meaner and quicker than the other guy. You can't pretend that you're prepared to kill him. You have to *be* prepared to kill him. And you have to be prepared to kill him even before he's started to think about what he feels on the subject.'

Now Earl looked round at the two townsmen. 'It's only afterwards that you get to think about it. It seems like a miracle that one man could get through that whole war, but a lot of us did. And sometimes it's hard to live with.'

'You never asked for any war,' Bob said.

'No. But I live with what I did and I live with what I learned. You boys were too young, I guess. You're lucky.'

'You ain't done anything wrong here, buddy,' George said. 'If that's what you're thinking. These guys started it all.'

Earl reached across the table towards George's makings. He rarely smoked and never carried any tobacco himself. It was another relic of the war. You didn't want to be craving a cigarette when you were lying on a tump just twenty yards from the enemy. But right now he had the urge to keep his hands busy and also to feel the burning of hot smoke in his lungs. 'May I?'

'Sure.'

'Last night I killed two men who didn't even know I was there. A lot of folks would call that cowardly.'

'They were setting to burn this place down,' Bob said. 'With the Laskies in it.'

'Nevertheless.'

'Nevertheless nothing,' George said.

'This afternoon I shot two more. I didn't even hesitate. I still carry Bean's lesson around with me.'

'If they'd had the drop on you what would have happened?' George said. 'I'll tell you. They'd have marched you down to Coleman's ranch and you'd have been hanging from his roof now. Or being dragged behind a horse till you were dead.'

'The war finished fifteen years ago.'

'This is a new war, Earl,' Bob said. 'And you never asked for this one either.'

Earl lit the cigarette he'd just rolled, took the smoke in and let it out again. It hung in a cloud around his face.

'You guys believe in God?' he said.

George and Bob looked at each other. They heard Earl get up and when they looked back at him he was staring out of the window again. 'I've found myself praying lately,' he said. 'But I'm not sure who to.'

The new war that Bob Forrest had mentioned started in earnest an hour after dawn the next morning. Earl heard the sound of thunder created by a thousand head of cattle rolling across the plain towards him and he saw the huge cloud of dust rising upwards causing the low sunlight to break into hundreds of long beams, all moving and shimmering, all darkening as the stampeding herd came closer and closer.

'Time to rise and shine,' he said to Bob and George, who were sleeping in Mrs Laskie and Elizabeth's cots respectively, both having stood watch for three hours each earlier.

'What is it?' George said sleepily, but already registering the low rumble and the tremble of the earth.

'It's Coleman.'

Bob Forrest pressed his palms into his eyes and then wiped his hands down his face. 'Sounds like about a thousand Colemans,' he said, standing up.

'We'd better make ourselves scarce,' Earl said. 'Get up on the rise out back and keep out of the way.'

'He's going to flatten everything,' George said.

'Uh-huh.'

'Good job you got the Laskies out of here,' Bob said.

Earl recalled telling Mrs Laskie that when all of this trouble was over the farm would still be here for her, if she wanted it. Now it seemed that his words were going to be proved a lie. If there were as many cattle out there as it sounded like then this farm – crops, fences, even buildings – was going to be as flat as when the Laskies had first arrived.

'It's wrong,' Earl said.

'What is?'

'That one man can do this, can ruin somebody this way. Destroy a family and a home just for the sake of pride.' His melancholy of the previous day was long gone. He'd lain awake on George's watch thinking of Jessica and the images had, as they always did, kept him from sleep, but at some point the rationalization was made that he wasn't in the wrong, that such men as those who killed his wife and the ones who had killed Mrs Laskie's husband had what was coming to them whether it came from a hidden rifle on a hill, or from fast guns in front of them.

'Pride comes before a fall,' Bob said, and the three of them slipped outside, took their horses up the east slope and hid out in the same gully where Earl had watched over the Laskies.

The entire plain below them seemed to be moving. At first it was possible to pick out the head of the stampede, a fast moving line of steers rolling across the earth like a flash flood sweeping through a canyon. It was even possible to pick out Coleman's men riding along the edges of the herd, several times hear their whoops and hollers and once even a gunshot. As the controlled stampede came closer and the dust rode higher and thicker the morning became more dusk than dawn, and as the first steers smashed through Bud Laskie's half completed fence there was nothing to be seen but a mighty rolling flesh seemingly all the way back to the horizon.

The first wave of Longhorns swarmed either side of the Laskie dwelling and started to break to the left and right. Gun shots turned those that were heading south back on themselves and suddenly there wasn't enough room and the house itself was squeezed by hundreds of tons of cattle.

Now there were more gunshots, more *yee-has* and hollers, the sound of wood cracking and the screech and scream of steers being crushed against the building and sliced against broken glass from the windows. The thunder continued to rise in volume. Earl was sure they must be able to hear this terrible din all the way in town. Now it was nigh on impossible to see what was happening below them. Above them the sun broke through the dust cloud in places giving everything a strange unreal look. It was as if the whole world was on fire but without emitting any heat.

For minute after minute the destruction went on. At one point Earl looked to his right and saw that both Bob and George had pulled their neckerchiefs over their mouths and noses. All he could see were eyes squinting against the dust cloud. Something crashed to the ground below and following it, for the first time, the noise seemed to relent slightly, almost as if the huge crash had been some kind of climax to which the herd had been working. For the first time in an age it was possible to distinguish the individual sound of cattle's feet pounding the floor and the bellow from their lungs. There was more shouting, laughter, even, but now the sound was noticeably lessening. Earl thought of the first time he had seen and heard a locomotive roar by close up. This had been like that, only twenty times louder, fifty times more destructive, and the silence that followed seemed to be several hundred times more hollow.

Coleman's men were racing after the herd now, somehow trying to turn it, like one huge beast being urged round in a great circle by the jabbing of tiny pins in its massive flank. Earl knew that sooner or later the cattle would be gathered and returned to wherever they had been grazing before being used as a tool of Coleman's destruction. And however hard the task of turning and reforming the herd was it would pale into insignificance against the task of returning the Laskie spread to its former glory. In fact, he suspected that Mrs Laskie would never return. Her husband was dead; her home ruined: this wasn't a job or indeed a place for a widow.

Through the swirling dust, Earl could see that the buildings weren't just ruined, they were gone, crushed and flattened into their component parts, just the diamond glints of broken glass twinkling through the darkness to remind watchers of the effort and attention that Bud Laskie had once lavished on his modest home. The few possessions that the Laskies had left behind had vanished, destroyed beneath the feet of the herd. Fences had been smashed into kindling. Water barrels crushed. The creek beyond the house was muddied and the mud spread across the land. That was the one thing that would return to normal in hours. The mud would dry and the creek would flow clear by noon. But beyond the creek the fields that Bud Laskie had laboriously worked for several years, de-stoning, ploughing, irrigating, harvesting, over and over again, had been churned up until they were unrecognizable as fields.

The dust hung heavy in the air. To his right Bob Forrest pulled down his neckerchief and said, 'I ain't ever seen anything like that in my whole darn life.'

'I saw a train derailed in the war,' Earl said. 'It was going pretty fast when we blew up the tracks. It reminded me of that, I guess. But this went on a lot longer.'

'Mrs Laskie . . .' George Clancy said, but never completed the sentence. They all understood that there were no words that would cover how she'd feel when she saw what had happened to her farm.

In the distance the herd was like a huge black lake moving across the land. They could still feel the tremble of hoofs coming through the ground. But now there was something else, too. Lighter hoofs. A rider somewhere close. Very close.

Earl worked the action on his Winchester and down below to the left they heard an echo as the new rider worked his action too.

Earl put a finger to his lips and he, Bob and George all slid a little deeper into the hollow in which they were concealed. Down below, a rider emerged slowly from the dust. He too had a neckerchief over his mouth, a wide brimmed hat pulled low, and a rifle in his hand. He stopped his horse below them and looked directly at where they were hiding.

'What train would that have been you boys were talking about?' he said. 'The reason I ask, I had a lot of friends killed in a train that the rebs blew clean off the tracks.'

Thomas Coleman paced back and forth across the dining-room letting the rage and pain over Jared's death – and the death of his other men – alternate with a warm and exciting feeling of coming vengeance. He poured himself a whiskey from the decanter on the sideboard and downed most of it in one swallow. He lit a cigar. He stood by the window and looked out at the hills against which he'd built this house. Beyond the hills, out of sight, was the Laskie farm. He glanced across at the tall clock standing in the corner of the room. No, the Laskie farm would be levelled by now provided everything had gone according to plan. The thought gave him little comfort or joy. Things had gone beyond the Laskies now. In itself, the destruction was no more than tying up a loose end, a symbolic act to show anyone who cared to look that Coleman kept his word. But it didn't mean anything. Peg Leg Laskie was dead. Maybe his family was too, though he suspected they'd have had time to escape before the herd hit them. But would the farm have still meant anything to them anyway? He doubted it. Having a man – even a one-legged man – about the place was a necessity. With no husband he suspected that Mrs Laskie would have upped and gone anyway.

He finished the whiskey in one more swallow, enjoyed the burning as it went down and let that fire mingle with his hatred for Earl Navarro. He wanted that man more than he'd wanted anything else in his whole life. At least it felt that way right now. And, by God, he'd always got what he'd wanted. He found himself at the sideboard pouring more alcohol into his glass. He'd told his boys that it wouldn't be enough to kill Navarro and he doubted he'd ever said a truer word. The man needed to suffer for what he'd done. The man would suffer. And when he believed that he'd endured all the suffering that a person could endure then he would suffer some more.

Only then would Coleman kill him.

He drank more whiskey and then he looked at the clock again. He had faith in his boys and he had faith in his own plan.

For Earl Navarro the end was coming.

*

Earl looked down at the newcomer. The man had a still-
ness and a confidence about him that Earl instinctively
liked. He showed no fear and he'd ridden right up and
addressed Earl, Bob, and George in their hiding place so
he had good eyes and a good nose, too. He had a rifle in
his hand – a cocked rifle, Earl knew that from the sounds
of a few seconds before – and he wore a six-gun on his hip.

But he was a Yankee.

'You got nothing to say about killing all my friends?' the
Yankee asked.

After a moment's thought Earl said, 'I had a wife.
Prettiest girl you ever saw. Some yellow Yankees cut her
throat whilst I was away fighting.'

The two men stared at each other for several long seconds
more. The dust all around them showed little sign of settling.
The light had taken on a strange orange hue as the sunlight
tried to find a way through the heavy atmosphere.

Eventually the Yankee said, 'There were some bad ones
on both sides.'

'Are you still fighting?' Earl asked.

'We won, didn't we? Why would I still be fighting? Are
you?'

Earl studied the man. 'You're Frank, aren't you?'

'How d'you know?'

'Your sister told me she'd written you.'

'She said they were in trouble over land. I aimed to
surprise them this morning.' He looked across to his left.
'They weren't in there, were they? I can't imagine Bud out-
running a stampede.'

'Bud's dead.'

Frank thought about this for a moment. 'And my
sister?'

'She's in town. We persuaded her to leave yesterday.'

'You knew something was going to happen?'

'Yep.'

'We got a lot to talk about,' Frank said. 'How about we lower our rifles and call a truce?'

Earl lowered his rifle. 'This is Bob Forrest and George Clancy.'

'Frank Murray. Please to meet you fellows.'

'You too,' Bob Forrest said.

'Frank,' George Clancy said.

'So Bud's dead and Jeannie's house has just been crushed beneath a thousand head of Longhorns. You guys going to tell me which way I ride and who I kill when I get there?'

CHAPTER SIX

Old Man Gallagher leaned his head back against the barbershop timbers and looked out beyond the town limits to the plain and the mountains in the distance. He fancied he could see the dust cloud from the stampede out there but the truth was the only dust he could see was that raised by a couple of dozen townsfolk – including all the remaining Laskies and Sheriff Garvey – heading out to the Laskie ranch to see if what the man said was true. There was a time when Gallagher would have been the first one out there. Well, maybe not the first, but he'd have certainly borrowed a ride in somebody's buggy to have a look for himself. But these days he was happy to smoke his pipe and let his imagination and other people's reports do the work.

The young man had ridden in earlier that morning. A dollar to a dime he was one of Coleman's men. Gallagher hadn't seen this fellow before. At least he didn't think so. But that didn't mean anything. Those cowboys never seemed to stay too long in one place.

'Morning,' Gallagher had said as the young man had ridden by.

'Morning,' the fellow had said, slowing.

'What brings you to town?' Gallagher said, holding his hands up in an innocent gesture in case the fellow had taken offence. 'Just asking, like. It's what I do.'

'I've got a message.'

'Who for?'

The young man paused. Gallagher could sense him weighing up his options.

'It's just I can probably point you in the right direction,' Gallagher said.

'I don't rightly know,' the man said. 'I was out to the west. There was a stampede.'

Gallagher leaned forwards.

'Someone's farm got hit pretty bad.'

The young man was lying. There wasn't any need for him to be out there unless he was working for Coleman in which case he'd know exactly whose farm it was. There was only one farm out there these days. Coleman had swallowed up all of the others long ago.

'A place by a creek?' Gallagher asked.

'Yep. You know it?'

'It's the Laskie ranch.'

'I sure hope they weren't in there. I just figured I ought to come tell someone.'

Gallagher looked at the gun on the young rider's hip. He decided against recommending that the fellow go and tell the story in Gillespie's. The townsfolk were already riled. They'd see through this fellow quicker than a woodsman saw through a tree. They'd likely kill him the way things were. But he'd likely kill a couple of them too.

'You might want to go and knock on Sheriff Garvey's door,' Gallagher said. 'Just down the street on the right.'

'Thank you. I'll do that.'

Gallagher watched him ride off and then he reached behind and rapped his knuckles on the barbershop window.

'What is it, Amos?' Nathaniel said from the doorway.

'Young feller down there just told me that Coleman sent all his cattle through the Laskie place. It's been destroyed.'

'Earl Navarro's out there,' Nathaniel said.

'Aye. Bob Forrest and George Clancy too.'

After that the story ripped though town like a locust storm and it wasn't long before half the townsfolk were saddling up and heading out to see what had happened.

It was a ready-made diversion. Not a massive one, but it was enough. Those folk who hadn't ridden to the Laskie farm were out on the street talking about it. Wesley Coleman and Andreas waited for Cal to leave town, riding out the east side and circling back to where they waited, then they hobbled the horses about 500 yards from the town limits and simply walked up to the back of Louisa Glanton's boarding-house.

An old wagon with a broken wheel and two empty water barrels marked the boundary of Louisa's property. A washing-line ran from a hook in one of the rear timbers of the house through to a post that had been driven into the hard ground just in front of the busted wagon. There were clothes on the line.

The men crouched behind the wagon.

'I'm going to have a look through the window,' Wesley said. 'Cal, you keep an eye out. Just call – but quietly – if we need to run. Andreas, if I give you the signal I want you to cut the line by the post then get back behind the wagon.

You keep out of sight too, Cal.'

Both men nodded and Wesley quietly slipped through the yard and up to the rear window of the boarding-house. There were just two rooms, and from one of them you could see clear through to the street on the far side. There was a large table covered in a white cloth with lace edging, two comfortable-looking chairs, a sideboard supporting a large oil lamp and several silver ornaments, a picture and a mirror on the wall, and curtains. It looked cool and inviting. It had a woman's touch. But there was no woman in there. Maybe she was out on the street with the rest of them. Maybe she'd even hitched a ride out to the Laskie place. That would mean a rethink – or at least a long wait. Wesley edged along the rear of the property and peered through the second window. The kitchen. This room only slightly smaller than the other. It had a table, but this one more solid and uncovered. There was a large stove up against the wall. A pot was simmering on the stove. This close Wesley could smell the cooking. Meat stew. It smelled good. Louisa Glanton was stirring the stew.

She was a fine-looking woman, Wesley thought. A good figure. Not too skinny like some women but not too big like others. She had her hair tied up and a few tendrils fell loose against her smooth neck. She wore a blue apron over a long dark-red dress. She lifted the spoon and tasted the cooking, smiled, and then rocked her shoulders left and right as if she was hearing music inside her head.

He eased back from the window and nodded towards Andreas.

Andreas stepped forwards, pulled out a knife, and cut through Louisa's washing-line. Her drying clothes fell to the dirt.

Wesley wouldn't put it past a woman to have instincts that alerted her any time her washing was on the floor, but just to make sure he pulled a Colt .45 from his holster, reached across and tapped the kitchen window sharply, and then pressed himself low and hard up against the back wall of her house.

He tried to imagine the next few seconds. She'd look round from the pot, puzzled. In a moment or two she'd be looking out of the window. She'd see the washing on the floor and she'd probably cuss – though he couldn't imagine such a pretty woman cussing too hard – and then she'd coming flying around the corner, her apron and dress flapping as she ran.

And he'd be there waiting.

He eased the hammer back on the Colt. 45, then considered what his father would say if he shot and killed her by mistake, and let the hammer back down. Darn it, he should've made sure Cal and Andreas knew how important it was to keep her alive. Still, what could go wrong? Three armed men against one women.

Except it wasn't Louisa who came around the corner. Not first, anyway. What must have happened was when she saw the washing on the ground she must have cussed just as he'd imagined and some fellow who was in the house with her must have figured on helping her out. Probably trying to get into her good books, Wesley thought.

He was a tall fellow, skinny, in black trousers, suspenders and a white under-shirt. He had no shoes on his feet and no hat on his head. He only looked half-dressed. Maybe it was some of his clothes lying on the floor.

Then Louisa came running into sight, too.

Cal stood up from behind the wagon. Andreas, also. Both had guns in their hands. Wesley wanted to yell at them not to shoot but there didn't seem to be time. Instead he jumped forward towards the Glanton women. She saw him coming and opened her mouth to say something, or to yell, or scream and simultaneously the skinny fellow did open his mouth. He just managed to say 'What in the heck—' and then Cal shot him right in the heart, the explosion sounding louder than any other gunshot Wesley had ever heard, echoes reverberating against the house. The man fell in a heap on the floor. And then Louisa Glanton did scream, but Wesley clamped his hand over her mouth, his arm around her waist and began half-dragging half-carrying her across the yard and out to the clear land beyond.

'Help me,' he called. She was twisting and kicking like a young steer at branding time and scratching like a cat in a corner. Her apron was wrapped around his hand and he could feel his grip slipping. She bit his hand and he yelped. He wasn't sure but he thought he heard someone yelling way over in the street. 'Hit her,' he said, and her eyes widened. She thrashed about even more wildly. So far they'd barely made it twenty yards out of her yard.

Then Andreas came up, turned the Colt .45 the wrong way round in his hand, and tapped her just behind the ear.

It didn't look like a hard blow but she stopped struggling and became dead weight in Wesley's arms. He stopped momentarily, hoisted her over his shoulder and then set off running.

Bob Forrest went down to the creek, upstream of where

the herd had muddied it, and filled a pan with water. Down by the ruins of the Laskie house Earl set about building a small fire. Once he got the flames licking around the wood he turned to Frank.

'Before I tell you what's been happening you have to know that your sister's husband came to me for help,' Earl said. 'Originally,' he added, with some emphasis on the final word.

Frank, crouching down on his ankles, looked at him. Earl saw the sheen of toughness in the man's blue eyes, the grit of hard living that had roughened his skin. He had long dark hair, just above his shoulders. And there was that still-ness that Earl had noticed earlier; even hunkered down by the fire he was motionless, listening to Earl, watching Earl, taking it all in. Earl decided he wouldn't want to play cards with this fellow, then he changed his mind and thought how much he *would* like to play cards with Frank. It would make for a very interesting game. He started to wonder on how useful the fellow might be with the rifle he had drawn on them earlier, and also the six-gun he wore around his waist.

'And you refused,' Frank said, after a long thinking pause. It wasn't a question.

Earl nodded.

Frank picked up a sliver of broken wood and poked the flames. Bob was coming back up from the creek with the water and George Clancy was making a tripod of long sticks on which to hang the coffee pot over the flames.

'What happened?' Frank said, not looking at Earl now, instead his eyes were on the fire.

'I was drunk when he asked me,' Earl said. 'But that's not the reason. If I'd have been sober I'd have still said no. I've spent my whole life since the war being somebody or other's gun. I got tired of looking over my shoulder. I got tired of being the one risking my skin. I guess I just got tired, full stop.'

Frank nodded, still not looking at Earl.

'It was the wrong call,' Earl continued. 'A man like me. . . .' He paused and waited for Frank to look up. When the newcomer did so Earl went on, 'Men like *us*. We don't have that luxury, do we? We are what we are. We do what we do.'

Frank held Earl's gaze and said, 'Did you get scared?'

'Maybe. I guess a man who's not scared of dying never came close to it. It's not that, though. I know there's going to be a younger man turn up some day. A faster man. I mean, these things are practically antiques now.' He tapped one of his .44s.

'You should get a forty-five,' Frank said.

'Until the last few days I never planned on using them again.'

'So you turned Bud down. Then what?'

'A couple of days later they hanged him.'

'They?'

'Thomas Coleman and his crew.'

Frank nodded. 'Jeannie told me about Coleman in her letter.'

'Couple of days after the funeral they tried to burn her out.'

'They failed, I presume.'

'I was waiting. I felt guilty.' Earl paused, wondering whether Frank would say anything about guilt, but he didn't. Bob Forrest hung the pot of water above the fire. 'I killed two of Coleman's riders.'

Now Frank nodded, the makings of a smile on his lips.

'And so in retaliation . . .' He swept a hand at the carnage that surrounded them.

'Not quite.'

'There's more?'

Earl told Frank of how he'd set out on a reconnaissance mission to find out who he was up against, how he'd almost got caught and had killed another two of Coleman's men in the process of getting away.

'These guys came looking for me.' Earl nodded in the direction of George and Bob. 'They're good fellows. We managed to persuade your sister to retreat to town. Just in time as it happened. You saw the rest with your own eyes.'

'Jeannie tells me he only wants this land because he can't have it.'

'Apparently so.'

'So what's your plan?'

The water was boiling. George dropped some coffee beans in.

'I figure to take the fight to them. Show Mr Coleman what it's like to be burned out.'

'And you have a plan how you're going to do that?'

'Not exactly.'

Frank smiled. 'Not a strategist, huh?'

'I'll figure something out.'

'Listen, I was in over a dozen major battles. Helped plan the strategy for three of 'em. Before that I was a sniper. Maybe I can have a look round, too. How many men have you got?'

'You're looking at us.'

Frank pursed his lips. 'It's not always about manpower. Maybe you and I can take a ride back over to Coleman's place.'

'Just one thing,' Earl said. 'I'm not taking orders from no damn Yankee.' He smiled quickly to show he was joking.

Frank let the joke ride and said, 'You know, you could've lied to me about refusing to help my sister and I'd have never known.'

'It crossed my mind.'

'We're very much alike. I'd have probably refused, too. You can't spend your whole life helping out strangers.'

'I think maybe that I'm fated to do exactly that.'

'I'm not quick on the draw,' Frank said. 'But I can hit a silver dollar at three hundred yards and I've never lost a war yet.'

'Then let's have this coffee,' Earl said. 'And go and plan one.'

They were drinking the coffee and smoking cigarettes when the first of the townsfolk appeared silhouetted on top of the ridge. Whoever it was paused, maybe taken aback by the devastation below them. Someone else appeared on the skyline. Earl Navarro stood up, coffee cup in his left hand, his right hand free. He could shoot with either but his right hand was the stronger. Not that there was any danger from the group of people now appearing up there, but it was instinct more than anything that kept his hand hovering close to his gun. He wasn't even fully aware that he was doing it.

Sheriff Garvey broke loose from the crowd and brought his horse down the slope. Others followed. About six back came Jeannie Laskie with Elizabeth and John. Jeannie's face was white. Earl looked across at Elizabeth and felt that twist in his gut as if the years had suddenly folded back on themselves and he was looking at Jessica again. Then Jeannie spotted Frank and a smile broke free from her pale frown. She jumped down from the buggy she'd been driving and ran towards her brother, hugging him. Elizabeth glanced at Earl and smiled. John Laskie jumped down from the back of the buggy and started lifting pieces of wood and stone as if trying to find some remnant of their house that hadn't been destroyed. More people arrived and suddenly the four men were surrounded by townsfolk, all asking questions and swearing and spitting and cursing the Colemans and talking about getting a group up together and heading out to the Double C and seeing how *he* liked it.

Earl found himself looking up the ridge to see if Louisa was coming. Hell, of course she wasn't, he told himself. She didn't even have a horse. He realized he hadn't seen her for several days. Was it really that long? So much had happened it felt like longer. He thought back to the way her fingers had felt in his, to the way she smiled at him, the way she had told him she'd heard stories about how he'd given up his old life and had added, 'I'd hoped they were true.'

Quietly he edged his way out of the crowd of people and made his way back up the slope to where his horse was tethered. He'd head back to town, get a bath, eat some good food, get some sleep, and then he and Frank and maybe Bob and George would go and plan for this new war.

But first of all he'd see Louisa.

CHAPTER SEVEN

Old Man Gallagher said, hardly before Earl had got within hearing distance, 'They killed Mannie Beauvais and they took Louisa.'

'What?'

'Snuck up back of her house whilst just about everyone was out front talking about the Laskies.'

Earl felt a sickness in his heart and a rage in his head. 'How long ago was this?'

' 'Bout thirty minutes.'

'How many of them?'

He'd already started to turn his horse when Gallagher said, 'Three, best as anyone could make out.' Then Earl was racing back out of town, cutting across scrubland towards the west, up to the back of Louisa's where he reined the horse in, wheeled round and round looking at the tracks on the ground, followed them slowly, seeing where they'd walked, then where they'd left the horses, and now riding as fast as he could, following their trail.

Thirty minutes. It was too much. If he had half a day he'd catch them easy. But it was only two and half hours or so to get to the Double C – and he was certain that's where they'd be headed. It wasn't far enough. Although, unless he'd read the tracks wrong, they'd only brought three horses so one of them was two up. It would slow them a little. But then, they'd killed Mannie Beauvais, so they must know they'd be being chased, so they'd be pushing hard.

Earl gritted his teeth and spurred his horse on.

Louisa didn't know if it was the sound of the gunfire or the squeal of delight from one of the cowboys riding alongside her that finally brought her round.

'I got him!' the boy yelled. 'I killed the son of a bitch!'

She was face down watching the ground thunder by just a few feet from her face, the horse's hoofs looking as if they were going to smash into her face with every thrust of its legs. Her head felt as if an axe had cleaved it in two and an equally cruel pain was lancing through her body with every jerk of movement. She was tied to the back of someone's saddle like a sack of corn, her arms and legs bound together, the cantle digging into her side like a fist.

For a moment everything wavered and unconsciousness retook her. But it was only for a few blissful seconds before the sound of laughter brought her back again. The horse was slowing now, turning.

'I tell you I killed him,' the same boy cried. She could only see him from the waist down. It hurt too much to try and twist her head upwards.

'How sure are you?' the man riding the horse on which she was tied, said.

'I'm pretty sure.'

'Sure enough to go back and have a look?'

'He went clean off the back of his horse.'

'That's not what I asked.'

'If we all go . . .'

'Uh-huh. I'm taking the lady on. She's what we came for, not to check up on some dumb feller from town who decided to trail us. You go.'

'I don't know.'

'Come on,' another man said. 'We'll both go and take a look and catch up with Wes in a moment.'

'Go careful,' the one called Wes said. 'Pa doesn't want to lose any more men.'

'I'm pretty sure he's dead,' the first kid said, and then the cantle dug into her cruelly again as Wes turned and rode on.

Earl Navarro caught them far quicker than he'd antici-pated. He'd found a place where they'd stopped, lots of foot marks around one of the horses, and he'd guessed this is where they'd paused to tie Louisa onto one of the horses. Not long after that he saw them in the distance, three of them, not going fast, just steady by the look of it, towards the distant foothills. He pressed on, pushing his horse harder than he would have liked. He wondered had Frank been here how far away he'd be able to be and still take a sniper's shot at them. But he wasn't Frank and he needed to get closer.

Then they heard him coming. One of them twisting round in his saddle, saying something, pulling a rifle from a saddle scabbard. The one with Louisa tied over the back of his horse starting to gallop.

Earl pulled the Winchester from his own scabbard, worked the action, and gripping the horse with his knees exchanged shots with the cowboy. They were both too far away from one another to have much hope of success.

Now the boy raced forwards to first catch up then overtake his compatriots. Earl worked the action and fired again. The boy pulled his horse around, taking his time. Again Earl thought of Frank the sniper and suddenly instinct made him lean as far to the right as he could, putting as much of his horse between him and the cowboy as he could. He fired off another loose round and then the cowboy replied and instantly Earl felt the bullet plough into his left leg, which was kicked free of the stirrup, and a moment later, his balance all wrong where'd he'd been leaning across to the right for cover, he felt himself sliding off the horse, his right foot getting caught in its stirrup for twenty bone-crunching yards before it too slipped free and he lay there on the ground winded, the Winchester somewhere behind him.

Whilst Wesley Coleman pressed on towards the Double C with his precious female cargo bound to his horse, Cal and Andreas doubled back. Cal had a rifle in his hands, Andreas a .45. They only had to ride a little over 200 yards before they saw the horse belonging to the man who had been following them standing still about thirty feet from where the man lay motionless on the ground. He was 150 yards away.

'I can make sure from here,' Cal called across to Andreas.

'Do it,' Andreas said.

Both riders stopped. Cal raised his rifle and took careful aim on the man lying motionless in the distance.

Earl Navarro knew he had to get to his gun. His .44s didn't have the accuracy at range to get him out of this hole. He started to crawl and the pain in his leg brought him to a halt before he'd made six inches. He gritted his teeth and tried again. This time his whole body protested. He wasn't sure if he hadn't broken some ribs when he'd been bounced along the ground behind his horse, and on top of that, both arms and his head felt like they'd been on the wrong end of a kicking mule. He reached down to his leg. His hand came away slick with blood. He knew little about anatomy but had seen more than one man bleed to death in minutes after being shot in the leg. Reaching his Winchester would be of little consequence if he no longer had the strength left to aim and fire it. So, snarling with determination, he rolled over and tried to get a better look at the extent of his wound. The bullet had gone in through the front of his trousers just above the knee; reaching behind his legs he could feel the wet bloodied patch where it had come out. There was no way to know how bad it was. He glanced back up in the direction that the riders had gone. They were halfway to the horizon now. Maybe they weren't stopping. If it had been him he'd have circled back round to make sure. Then again, maybe Louisa was a prize that over-ruled all other decisions. At the thought of Louisa he swore aloud and rolled over onto his right-hand side. He undid the long lace that bound the bottom of his left holster to his thigh and he retied it an inch lower and much tighter.

Then he forced himself to start crawling back towards his rifle.

It seemed like an age before he made it, his face bathed in sweat and a trail of blood behind him. He rested his head on his hands for a moment and felt the distant tremble of horses hoofs on the ground.

Quickly he turned and sure enough two of the riders were coming back. He worked the action on the rifle, and he pressed himself hard into the earth.

The riders split up. Not too far apart that they couldn't communicate but far enough that it would be difficult to get off two accurate shots. Now they were slowing, stopping. And one of them was raising a rifle, probably the one who shot him earlier, Earl guessed. And with that thought he found himself conjuring up Frank the sniper once more. This time the image helped make his own aim steady as he sighted down the Winchester at the distant rider.

The bullet hit Cal in the shoulder, knocking his own aim way off. His finger pulled against the trigger of his rifle as he was knocked backwards and his bullet flew aimlessly into the clear sky. His horse whinnied and stepped backwards and somehow he managed to stay on, pulling himself upright by yanking hard on the reins and bringing the horse's forelegs briefly into the air.

'Cal?' Andreas called, but before Cal could answer another bullet took him clean in the throat and this one tore him right off the back of the horse and he was dead before he hit the dirt.

'Cal!' Andreas cried again, and then instinct took over and he was lying over his horse, wheeling it in a clockwise direction and racing across to his fallen comrade.

Another rifle bullet whistled through the air and now Andreas slid off the horse and scurried on all fours across to Cal. The dead man lay with his eyes open and a hint of surprise on his lips. The hole in his throat was small but the dirt behind him was already sodden with blood. The gunfire had spooked Cal's horse into retreating thirty or forty yards and now Andreas's mount whinnied nervously. With tears of rage filling his eyes, Andreas reached up and grabbed the reins to prevent his horse racing off too. He kept the horse between him and the man out there as he crouched down over Cal. It seemed impossible that his friend had been killed so easily.

Now he heard the whistle of another bullet shrieking through the air. The sound of the gun and the thump as the bullet hit home seemed to come simultaneously and for a moment he was puzzled that he felt no pain. Then in front of him his horse crumpled down onto its knees, rolled over, wheezing and snorting.

Andreas dived flat on the ground as yet another bullet whistled through the air. His mind was raging with anger at the man who had not only shot his horse but his friend as well. He scrambled across Cal's body and took his friend's rifle; his own was beneath the dead weight of his horse. Then he lay behind the still breathing animal and he took aim at the dark human mound in the distance.

Earl Navarro could just see the man's hat above the horse. Aiming at the crown of the hat he carefully squeezed the trigger. The rifle bucked against his shoulder and he saw an explosion of horse flesh as his bullet ploughed into the horse about two inches too low. Now the hat disappeared behind the horse's torso.

'Damn,' he said. It had been a calculated move shooting the horse. It prevented the man getting away but it also gave him cover. Talking of cover, Earl twisted around in the dirt. He'd ended up in a particularly bad place. There were a few thirsty-looking plants around but nothing that would stop a bullet. The thought of thirsty plants brought a dryness to his throat. His horse was standing thirty or forty feet away nervously pawing a front foot against the ground. Earl's water skin was hooked to the saddle; most of his ammunition, too. He only had the bullets that were in the gun and he'd already fired several of those. He didn't want to call the horse over – assuming it would come – for that might encourage the fellow over there to shoot it and then he'd be stuck. His leg was sending pulses of pain up into his thigh and belly and he knew he'd struggle to get back to town without a horse. Yet he couldn't lie here forever. Not without water. Not whilst still bleeding.

Not without cover.

A bullet exploded about three inches in front of Andreas's face and showered him with blood and fragments of horseflesh. The horse moaned and shuddered and Andreas wormed his way deeper into the earth behind the animal. The guy out there was a good shot. But he was also injured and he had no cover. Andreas figured that Wes would be back at the Double C any time now. Hell, they might even be within hearing distance of the shooting. All he had to do was sit tight and make sure the fellow out there didn't move and pretty soon Wes would be back with a couple more riders then they could pick off this man at their leisure. Maybe even take him alive and have some fun with him back at the ranch.

He squirmed a few inches to the right and reached up to where his canteen hung from his saddle. He popped the cork in his teeth and took a long swig of water.

There was no hurry.

Earl Navarro gritted his teeth and pulled the lace tighter

around his thigh. The wound was still bleeding. Just twisting around to do this simple task made him feel dizzy and a little sick. He knew he was going to have to do something soon. Lying here waiting for the fellow to raise his head again wasn't going to work. Maybe if he could get within pistol range of the guy he could find some advantage. At least it would give him a few more shots, and anyway, what other plan was there?

So he started to crawl.

The pain in both his leg and torso was intense but simply thinking of Louisa helped overcome that. Thinking about the way Coleman had obliterated the Laskies' ranch – the Laskies' *lives* – helped, too. And thinking back to all the times he'd had to overcome worse pain and greater danger did the rest.

Sweat rolled down his face and he was scared to look behind in case the amount of blood he was trailing behind him was too off-putting. At one point instinct made Earl pause in his crawling and raise the rifle. A moment later he saw the fellow's hat start to rise. A fly buzzed across Earl's face. He ignored it. He waited. The hat paused.

Earl shot a round plumb through the middle of and the hat spun backwards through the air as if it had been raised on a stick rather than a head.

That was OK. It would have been nice to see an explosion of blood and brains and hear the guy scream but raising the hat on a stick was exactly what Earl would have done. At least the guy knew Earl was still watching him along the barrel of his rifle.

Earl started crawling again. He had to work his way through the pain barrier again and finally he did look back. There was less blood than he'd feared – still a lot, but he'd seen men bleed more. The worst thing was he'd only gone ten yards – about the distance he'd originally crawled back to get his gun. He cursed under his breath and when he closed his eyes briefly it felt as if the world was spinning around him.

He opened his eyes and in the distance beyond his adversary he could see dust clouds.

Reinforcements from the Double C.

CHAPTER EIGHT

George Clancy and Bob Forrest rode back to town slowly and alone. They'd left the crowds out at the Laskie place and had watched Earl Navarro in the distance riding ahead, pulling away from them.

'Hurrying to get home,' George said.

'Maybe he's got someone there waiting.'

'One of Gillespie's girls, perhaps?'

'I think he's got someone else on his mind,' Bob said.

'Who you thinking of?'

'I ain't sure. I ain't even sure he knows hisself.'

A little while later George said, 'That was something else, wasn't it?'

'The stampede?'

'Yeah.'

'I ain't ever seen anything like that before.'

'Me either.'

'What about this Frank fellow?'

'He snuck up on us good, didn't he?'

'Yeah. He seem OK to you?'

'Yep.'

'Yeah, me, too,' Bob said. 'Seems to me that with him

and Earl together ol' Coleman might find himself in a spot of bother.'

'By the sounds of it back there half the townsfolk are ready to ride against him, too.'

'The fellow's just pushed everyone a little too hard.'

'By all accounts the guy's got more money than anyone else in the territories: you'd think he'd be happy.'

'Some folks are never happy.'

'You're right there.'

They rode on, the mountains behind them still hazy through the dust hanging in the air, the sky above them clear blue, and the town growing closer with each step. Pretty soon they could see Old Man Gallagher leaning against the barbershop watching their approach. He leaned forward as they approached. Then he did something that neither of them could ever recall happening before: he stood up to address them.

'Some fellows came into town whilst everyone was out at the Laskie place,' Gallagher said, repeating the story he'd told Earl almost word for word. 'They killed Mannie Beauvais, they took Louisa, and Earl's gone after them.'

'What?'

'That's what Earl said.'

'Where was this?'

So Gallagher explained again what had happened and George Clancy and Bob Forrest wheeled their horses and raced out of town. Gallagher leaned his head back against the boards of the barbershop and sucked on his pipe. Nothing was forthcoming and when he examined the pipe he found the flame had expired. He searched through his pockets for a lucifer or two and when he had the pipe glowing again he relaxed once more and looked out of town to the mountains beyond. He wasn't quite sure how old he was or even how long he'd been in town. Heck, sometimes he couldn't remember a time when he hadn't passed his days sitting right there talking to strangers, gathering gossip, and watching the world go by. But in all that time he'd never known a day like this one. Never ever.

Thomas Coleman smiled. When the smile caused his cheeks to hurt he opened his mouth and laughed. The girl was slung over the back of his boy's horse and, as a couple of the Mexicans swung the gate closed, Coleman could see her twisting and grimacing in pain. That was good. He wouldn't hurt her himself – well, not so long as Navarro did as he was asked – but it wouldn't do any harm to let her think otherwise.

Wesley rode across the yard in front of the main house and threw a couple of glances backwards, not at the girl, but at the plain out there where his dust hung in the air.

Coleman's laughter died.

He stepped down from the porch and walked forward to meet Wesley, reaching up to catch the horse's reins.

'Where are they?' he asked. The girl twisted her head and her eyes blazed at him through a thick mask of dirt. A weak noise came from her mouth. He ignored her.

'We were being followed,' Wesley said. 'Cal shot him. They both went back to make sure he was dead.'

'And?'

'I don't know. There was more shooting. I figured it was more important to bring the girl.'

'You did right, son,' Coleman said, looking at the girl again. Her eyes were closed now, but she was coughing, and with every spasm she groaned in pain. Coleman clicked his fingers at the Mexicans. 'Untie the girl,' he said. 'Take her round the back and ask Queenie to clean her up and give her some water. Then tie her up again.'

'I need to get back out there,' Wesley said

'I'll call up a few more boys,' Coleman said. 'How far away was this?'

'Only fifteen minutes. Just the other side of the bluffs.'

'I can't afford to lose any more. 'Specially not those two.' Coleman spat on the ground. 'I ought to raze that whole darn town to the ground.' He looked out across the plain. 'Fact is, once I've finished with Navarro then I might just do that.'

Less than five minutes later Wesley Coleman was riding back out, this time with three more Double C hands. They rode fast but they still cracked evil jokes and laughed, albeit a little nervously. They chewed wads of Copenhagen and spat juice out onto the dry ground. And now again they ran their fingers over their guns and yelled to one another of what they'd like to do to the guy who had killed Jared and Papa and then Perry and Joe. And in the absence of the man himself any townsperson would do.

'What you reckon's happening?' one of them asked, after they'd been riding for ten minutes and the sound of a rifle shot reached them.

'I guess the man Cal shot isn't dead,' Wesley said.

'Let's hope not,' someone else said. 'We got a pole waiting for him.'

This brought a round of agreement and laughter.

'We better spread out,' Wesley said. 'I mean real far. By the sounds of it there's still plenty of life left in him.'

'For now.'

'Yeah, for now.'

The riders started to separate. Two to the left, one to the right, Wesley carrying on straight ahead. No one needed any telling what was out there. Cal had shot a man good enough that he thought the guy was dead. He and Andreas had gone back to check, and neither of them had reappeared. Shots still echoed out infrequently. So the guy was still alive, he had a gun and no doubt some cover. Coming at him from several directions he would be taken easily, dead or alive. It didn't really matter which. It was just a matter of doing it then getting back to the Double C for some chow.

George Clancy and Bob Forrest heard the shots before they saw anything. Even as they glanced at one another in concern they were pulling rifles out of saddle scabbards and spurring their horses onward. Then, as they topped a small rise, they could see in a glance the trouble that Earl Navarro was in. His horse lay dead and it looked liked he was trying to crawl towards it for cover. No, on second thoughts it wasn't Earl's horse that was dead, he was crawling towards a guy lying behind his own dead horse about fifty yards in the distance.

'Jeez,' Bob said, raising his gun and firing a wild shot towards the distant man more as an announcement of their presence than with any hope of hitting him.

'Look yonder,' George said. And Bob saw four more riders, splitting into pairs, heading towards them.

'Come on!' Bob said, leaning low over his horse's neck and urging it forward.

George knee-gripped his horse as hard as he could and fired two shots in the general direction of the approaching riders. On the ground ahead of them Earl fired too. One of the horses coming towards them reared up on its hind legs, the rider managed to stay on, but when the horse came back down its forelegs seemed to crumple beneath it and now the rider slipped off its side.

'He's hurt,' Bob cried, his voice breathless and shaking from the gallop. 'Can you keep them occupied?' He wasn't even sure George had heard.

Bullets were coming in their direction now, smoke puffing from the distant guns, the whistle of lead through the air arriving before the sound of the cartridges going off.

There was another man close by the one who had taken cover behind his horse. He was lying unmoving on the ground.

'Looks like he's killed another of them,' Bob said, more or less to himself. He'd never killed a man in his life whilst Earl Navarro seemed to do so wherever he went. The idea of killing someone brought a sick feeling to his stomach. He knew if he thought about it too much he'd never be able to do it. But there wasn't time for thinking. Their horses kicked up dust and the cowboys riding toward them kicked up dust. The sun blazing down out of a dusty sky seemed to make his face burn hotter than it had ever been and there wasn't time to watch what everyone was doing, or even to try and duck out of the way of the red hot lead whistling through the air. He could hardly catch his breath as his horse, which seemed to be galloping faster than it had ever done before, jarred him with every stride. He raised his gun and fired several shots though it was impossible to keep the gun steady, impossible to aim – something that he guessed later was why he was still alive as no doubt it was also happening to those cowboys coming toward them; only Earl and the other guy on the ground seemed able to shoot with any accuracy and Earl was making sure that guy kept his head down. Bob's gun almost slipped from his hand but he caught it. Now he was within shouting distance of Earl.

To his left George had slowed his horse and was taking more time with his shots. The guy whose horse had just been shot was lying behind it. The other fellow on that side had slowed to a halt and was now back tracking, crouched right over the side of his pony as George sent bullets whistling toward him. Earl Navarro fired another one at the man lying behind the horse in front of him and Bob aimed and fired at the two riders still coming up on his right.

'We got to get out of here,' he said to Earl.

Earl pressed the butt of his rifle into the ground and made it up onto his knees.

'Come on,' Bob said; his horse was alongside Earl now. He was watching the guys to the right. They were slowing, not keen to get too close, but in the process were getting a more stable platform for their shooting. Bob worked the lever and sent another bullet whistling their way. He threw a glance back at Earl Navarro. The man was still in the same position.

'You've got to get up,' he said. 'Here.' He held out his hand.

Earl reached up and took it and only then did Bob notice all the blood on his friend's clothes.

'You ready? This is going hurt.'

'Let's go,' Earl said.

Bob heaved upwards. He wasn't strong enough to do this one-handed. A bullet caused his hat to fly from his head. Now he slipped his gun back in its scabbard and reached down with his other hand, grasping Earl's arm with both hands. Earl grunted and seemed to push upwards and then he was lying across the saddle in front of Bob. Bob shuffled backwards whilst simultaneously grabbing Earl's pants with his left hand and heaving him across the saddle. Then he turned and kicked the horse and they were away whilst over to the left George sat upright working his rifle to a red heat spraying bullets around the whole panorama in front of them, two to the right keeping those guys occupied, another to keep them men on the ground down, another to the left.

'Come on,' Bob cried, as his horse surged back towards town.

As he looked at George to give him the nod he saw a bullet take George right in the forehead. His friend's hat came off and it seemed that the whole back of his head went with it. For a moment time seemed to pause, and then George Clancy, already dead, simply toppled off the back of his horse onto the dry earth beneath him.

Louisa came round slowly. A Negro woman was wiping a cold cloth across her forehead.

'Lie still, missy,' the woman said.

The cold cloth and the soft touch of the woman's hands caused Louisa to close her eyes again. She recalled waking up briefly with her head hanging down by a horse's legs, dust in her mouth, a terrible pain in her stomach. She felt that pain now and she winced involuntarily. The woman immediately stopped applying the wet cloth to her forehead and when Louisa opened her eyes the woman said, 'I'm sorry.'

'It's OK,' Louisa said. 'My stomach.'

'They treat you rough,' the woman said, and Louisa didn't know if it was a question or a statement, so she simply nodded. Even that small movement sent waves of pain through her belly and chest. The woman held a tin cup to Louisa's lips.

'Water.'

Louisa sipped the water gratefully. Afterwards she leant back and closed her eyes again. Now she could remember someone saying that they'd killed somebody. That would have been someone from town who'd set out to follow them. And with that thought she recalled coming out into her backyard with Mannie Beavais and being jumped by someone. She pictured Mannie getting shot.

'Where am I?' she asked.

'You at Mr Coleman's ranch,' the woman said.

'He's kidnapped me.'

'I don't know.'

Louisa tried to sit up. She was lying on a soft bed. Her clothes had been loosened but not taken off. Every bone felt as if it was bruised. 'You have to help me get out of here,' she said.

'Is not going to happen,' a male voice, Mexican Louisa believed, said from over by the door. She turned her head and saw him now, standing there with a look of apology on his dark face. 'Mr Coleman said that when you wake we tie you up.'

He stepped forward and Louisa saw that he had a length of thin rope in his hands. She looked up at the woman. 'No, please. I won't try to escape. I promise.'

'You be OK,' the woman said.

'So long as your fellow's prepared to trade himself for

you,' the Mexican said.

'My fellow?'

'*Sí.*'

'I don't have a fellow.'

'Mr Navarrao, no?'

'Mr Navarro? He's not my fellow.'

'Mr Coleman think so. Anyway, maybe Mr Navarro come anyway. Mr Coleman hope so. For your sake.'

Then he was tying her hands together, still smiling apologetically, and she closed her eyes and prayed that Earl would be sensible enough not to come.

CHAPTER NINE

'No wonder we won the war,' Frank said. 'Soldiers like you on the other side.'

Earl looked up at him, gritting his teeth as the doctor pulled a thread through his leg.

'I mean, I snuck up on you like you were asleep earlier. You almost got yourself captured just yesterday and were lucky to escape. And now you've gone and got shot.'

'There wasn't anything lucky about not getting captured,' Earl said.

'Still, I find it hard to figure out how you've stayed alive so long out here.'

'I got shot today because I was the only one who realized what was happening. Everyone else was busy playing happy families.'

Now Frank grinned, standing above him as the doctor stitched up the wound on Earl's leg. 'I'm just joking, Earl. Trying to take your mind off the doc's work.'

The doctor looked up. 'I'm all done now.'

'See?' Frank said. 'It worked.'

Earl said, 'If I didn't think you were serious about the joking the doc here would have some work to do on you.'

'Can you get up?' Frank said.

' 'Course I can,' Earl said, but when he tried to move his leg there was no strength in it. He tried again and pain lanced up into his thigh.

'Blood loss,' the doc said, closing his bag and slipping his spectacles into an inside pocket. 'Nothing plenty of water, food, and rest won't cure.'

'And there was me thinking it was old age,' Frank said, and Earl pulled a face at him.

'Come and see me in a fortnight and I'll remove the stitches if you've not pulled them out before then,' the doctor said. 'Good day.'

Now Frank helped Earl into a sitting position. They were in an upstairs room at Louisa's boarding-house. No sooner had the doctor gone than there was a knocking at the door and Bob Forrest came in.

'How'd it go?' Bob's face still had the greyness to it that had come over him like a cloud when he had seen George Clancy killed.

Earl nodded. 'I'll live.'

'Some of the boys are going out there to bring . . . to bring George home.'

Earl nodded. 'Tell them to be careful.'

'I'm going, too.'

'You don't have to.'

'I want to.'

'Don't go starting anything, Bob.'

'Someone's gotta pay for this, Earl.' There was a sheen of tears in Bob's eyes.

'Someone will pay. But let's do it on our own terms.'

Frank said, 'I'm going too, Earl. You heard what the doctor said. Rest and water.'

'Well, you guys just help me over to Gillespie's. I'll rest

98

and water myself over there whilst you fellows are riding around the countryside. And when you get back we'll talk about going to get Louisa.'

'You see, Miss Glanton,' Thomas Coleman said, 'I'm not a bad man. Not *evil*. I just know what I want and I go and get it.'

'Like killing Bud Laskie?'

'Please, I thought better of you. Bud Laskie was drunk and it was he who attacked my boys. He brought it on himself.'

She looked up at him, her hands tied in her lap. She wanted to spit on him. They were on the back porch of his ranch house looking out over the stables and the bunk house, the tack rooms, the smoke house, the corral where two dozen or more horses were held, and beyond that another fenced off area where a young cowboy had roped a horse and was walking it around and around. She was able to lift her hands to her mouth and there was a jug of water and a cup in front of her. She'd not touched either, yet.

'You hanged him,' she said. 'They said his good leg was shot and his false leg was broken. He brought all that on himself?'

'When a man gets shot at he's liable to react in any number of ways, Miss Glanton. Please don't judge my boys so badly for the way they reacted against a man who was trying to kill them.'

'I'm not judging your boys: I'm judging you.'

He smiled, then reached out and filled her cup with water. 'I know you're trying to be stubborn and refuse any hospitality I show, but please. . . .' He held out the cup to her.

She stared at him. 'You tried to burn out the Laskies before you killed him. You ruined their house by all accounts afterwards.'

Still he held the cup out towards her. 'Have you seen the ranch?'

'No. The word in town was that it was all gone.'

'Don't believe everything you hear.'

'Mrs Laskie herself told me about the fire.'

'The Laskies had been offered a vast sum of money. A vast sum for that land. More money than they'd see in a lifetime normally. They were fools not to accept it.'

'It was their land.'

Now he put the cup down.

'It's not easy being a man such as myself, you know.'

'I feel so sorry for you.'

'Sarcasm doesn't become you, Miss Glanton. Do you know how hard I've had to work to achieve all of this?' He swept a hand in front of him. 'And this is only part of what I own. I have similar in Texas. I lost a wife and a daughter to measles, a son to Navajo.'

'And you'd give it all up to have them back,' she said, still with the sarcasm in her voice.

He smiled again, this time thinly. 'Actually, no I wouldn't. I have other sons.' He stopped then and looked away briefly. He squeezed his eyes with his thumb and forefinger and for a moment she thought he was about to cry. Eventually he looked back up, composed again. 'I have another wife, albeit Indian. She's in Texas at the moment. I have cousins and nephews and brothers and sisters. My boys are like my family, too. So, no, I wouldn't give this up for anything. I've spent a lifetime building my business and I've not finished yet.'

'Not until you own the whole state.'

'Not even then.'

'Surely there will come a point when you can say enough's enough?'

He sipped his own water now, leaned back in his chair and took a cigar from his breast pocket.

'Maybe. Maybe not. It hasn't happened yet.'

'And you can't bear it when someone doesn't bow down before you.'

He bit the end off his cigar.

'I'm a fair man. In fact,' – he waved the hand holding the cigar out in front of him again – 'I pay these boys more than any other cattleman. They make a fortune from me. That's how fair I am.'

'I bet they don't cross you, though.'

'They have no need to cross me.'

'And if they did, like the Laskies you'd just destroy them.'

Still he looked at her, his cigar unlit.

'You can't bear to have people stand up to you, can you?'

Now he took out a match, flicked it with his thumbnail, lit the cigar, and breathed smoke into the air between them.

'Sometimes I enjoy the challenge,' he said. 'But I always give folks an opportunity to settle things, shall we say, peaceably, first.'

Now she finally reached out and picked up the cup of water he'd poured.

'And Earl Navarro?' she said.

This time his rare smile was wider. Then it straightened as he said, 'He's killed four of my boys already. Maybe another, too. But his time is up.'

'You think he's going to come?'

'I know he's going to come. I've sent a boy out there already to tell him.'

'He'll kill you.'

'No. He was a worthy adversary for a short while; now it's time for him to pay for what he's done.'

She raised the cup of water to her lips.

'Drink up,' he said.

And she threw it over his face, smiling as the cigar sizzled out, not caring that he lashed out and knocked her off the chair; sunlight and shadows combining to make it appear as if a wild animal's face existed just beneath his own.

'Maybe I'll force you to watch,' he said, storming off the porch, calling for someone to lock her up.

Earl sat at a table in the rear of Gillespie's trying and failing to concentrate on the deck of cards he was shuffling and dealing out to himself. Annie was at the bar talking to Gillespie. A couple of fellows were rolling dice and betting on the outcome at a table by the door and a dog was scratching himself out on the plank-walk just beyond. Earl had ordered a whiskey, downed it in one, then ordered another. Gillespie had asked him about George Clancy, said he'd heard a rumour that George had been shot dead. Earl had told him that the rumour was true and that a couple of the boys had gone out to get the body and when they got back they were going to decide on what their next move would be.

'Basically, we're going to go out there and kill Coleman,' Earl said.

'He's got Louisa,' Annie said. There was no make-up on her face and she looked pale and ghostlike standing there in the dark interior of the bar.

'Temporarily,' Earl said.

'And it was Coleman who shot you?' Gillespie asked.

'As good as. One of his boys. He's dead now.'

Earl downed his second whiskey and ordered a third, this time forcing himself to walk to the bar to collect it. One of the dice players looked up. 'If there's anything we can do, Earl.'

'Thanks, Sonny. We might be raising an army yet.'

'Something we should have done years ago,' Gillespie said. 'You can't have folks like Coleman just coming along and taking anything they want.'

'He won't be for much longer,' Earl said. He picked up his drink and limped back across to the table in the corner of the room. It felt like there was an arrowhead buried in his leg but he knew the whiskey would help, and anyway the pain made him think of Louisa and George and Bud Laskie and Mannie Beauvais.

After a couple more hands of solitaire Gillespie walked across and placed another whiskey in front of Earl. 'That's on the house,' he said. 'Sonny's got you one, too.'

'Much obliged fellows,' Earl said. Time seemed to pass very slowly. He couldn't help but wonder what Coleman was doing to Louisa. God help the man if he laid one finger on her.

A few men came into the bar and ordered drinks. They looked over and nodded at Earl. Then they asked him about George and also about how he'd got shot himself. The doc called in and chastized Earl for drinking whiskey so soon after his injury. 'It thins the blood, Earl,' he said.

'You need feeding up with food not filling up with whiskey.'

'The lady who cooks my food is missing right now,' Earl said, the alcohol running fast through his thinning blood.

A little later Sheriff Garvey came in. He and Earl exchanged stares for a moment. Garvey was a short fellow with higher than normal heels on his boots. Earl recalled Bud Laskie saying that Garvey was either a coward or in Coleman's pocket. He knew the sheriff wasn't a coward. He'd seen the man break up fights and face-down armed drunkards. It didn't necessarily follow that the man was taking money from Coleman but something paid for his custom-made boots and he'd been notable in his lack of action towards Coleman these last few days.

'Sorry to hear about what happened out there,' Garvey said.

'Which bit?'

Garvey continued to stare at Earl. 'All of it. You getting shot, George getting murdered, Louisa. . . .'

'Are you going to ride out to the Coleman place, see if she's there?'

Garvey paused before saying, 'I don't have any jurisdiction out there. But I will go; I would have gone before, I was out at the Laskie place.'

'You might want to ask Mr Coleman about that whilst you're out there.'

Garvey made to say something, paused, and then said, 'Don't underestimate what I do for this town.'

'I know exactly what you do for this town.'

'You appear to dislike me, Mr Navarro. I only came in to express my concern over your injury and to thank you for what you've tried to do.'

Earl, too, held his tongue despite the whiskey trying to persuade him otherwise. He nodded. 'Your concern is appreciated, Sheriff. And what I've tried to do is only the start. Can we count on your help?'

'For what?'

'For whatever we decide to do.'

'So long as it's legal.'

Earl smiled and raised his glass to the sheriff, but said no more. When the sheriff left the saloon a ripple of animated conversation arose, but Earl paid it no heed. He was tired of people talking to him about this. He wanted to act not talk. He dealt out another hand of cards and tried to switch himself off from the sounds all around when a shadow fell over his table.

'I've come to say sorry,' Jeannie Laskie said. She looked around the room. 'Not just to you, but to everyone.' She was dressed in a clean blue dress and had a cream shawl around her shoulders. Her face was pale.

Looking up at her Earl was suddenly more conscious than ever of all the whiskey he'd drunk. In Jeannie Laskie's face he saw her daughter Elizabeth and that, in turn, made him think of Jessica.

'There's nothing to be sorry for, Mrs Laskie. Nothing at all.'

'If we . . . if we had just. . . .'

'Anything that's happened – and there's been plenty – can be laid at the feet of one man. We both know who's to blame here.'

'Nevertheless. We brought you into this.' She looked away from Earl and let her eyes wander over all the people in Gillespie's. 'We brought you all into this. And now Louisa's been kidnapped and George Clancy is dead. That other fellow, Mannie, too.'

'And you've lost a husband and a home,' Earl said.

Now there were tears in her eyes. 'Sometimes I wished we'd just taken the money and gone someplace else.'

Earl reached up and took her hand.

'When it's time to make a stand it's time to make a stand,' he said. 'You'd have never felt good about taking that man's money.'

'Nevertheless. . . .'

'Nevertheless nothing. There's one man who has to pay for all of this. And he's going to pay, trust me on that.'

She nodded, then reached up and wiped an eye.

'I don't like all this killing,' she said. 'But you're a good man, Earl Navarro.'

After she'd left Earl found it hard to concentrate on the cards again. He was wondering where Bob and Frank had got to, whether they'd picked up George Clancy's body or whether Coleman had pulled a fast one and snatched it away.

He downed the last of his drink and carefully lifted his leg – which had been resting horizontally on a chair to ease the pain – and was just about to stand when the doors to the saloon swung open again and a young stranger walked in. Within moments he was followed by Old Man Gallagher, the importance of whose appearance was not lost on Earl who could scarcely recall the man moving so rapidly before. The young man's face was flushed and dusty from fast riding. There was a gun at his hips and a sneer on his face. But he looked nervous. Scared, even.

'I've got a message from Mr Coleman,' he said. 'A message for Earl Navarro.'

CHAPTER TEN

Thomas Coleman had given Paul Chambers no choice about going into town and passing on the message to Earl Navarro.

'It's an order,' Coleman had said. 'But at the same time, I'll give you a week's wages just for doing it. How does that sound?'

That was one thing about Coleman, Chambers thought. He could be a hard man, a cruel man for sure – especially if you crossed him – but he was also a fair man. And he paid better than just about anybody else.

But was a week's wages worth it? Everybody at the Double C knew exactly what Navarro had done. He seemed to be a one-man killing machine, though a few of the hands had pointed out that he'd shot Jared and Papa Davey from a hidden position when neither of them had known he was there, and the fact was anybody could do that. He'd got lucky again with Perry and Joe and if it had been Navarro in that shootout this morning then although he killed Cal he took a bullet himself and one of the men who'd come to help Navarro got killed too. So, all in all, he wasn't that special. He was just sneaky. That's what the boys in the bunk house were saying, anyway. But it wasn't them who had to go and pass on Coleman's message.

Coleman told him to go the long way round. 'Don't take the direct trail where Cal got shot. And don't go by the Laskie place,' he said. 'There's liable to be townsfolk at either – or both. Just take it steady and when you get there you ask for Navarro and give him the message just as I told you. You got that?'

Chambers said he did. Coleman made him repeat the message back.

'OK. Off you go, son. And don't worry, so long as you tell them what I've told you to say they won't dare harm you.'

Chambers stopped and vomited in fear once out of sight of the ranch. After that he felt a little better. And in the cooling heat of the day he entered the town and asked the old-timer on the plank walk where he could find Navarro. The man was full of questions and Chambers had to let him know he was bringing a message from Coleman before the old fellow had told him where Navarro was at.

'He's in Gillespie's saloon,' the old-timer said. 'I would-n't like to be in your boots, son. Not when you tell him you're a Coleman boy.'

Then the old fellow pushed himself upright and hurried along the plank-walk trying to keep pace with Chambers.

Chambers tied his horse to the rail outside the saloon, hitched up his pants, straightened his hat, pulled his gun down against his thigh, swallowed, and went inside.

The alcohol drained away from Earl's blood making him feel as if he'd been following the doc's orders and taking water not whiskey. He drew one of his guns holding it low alongside his good thigh.

He let the kid stand there for a moment longer, the fear of uncertainty growing in his expression. No one anything.

'Earl Navarro,' the kid said again. 'I'm looking for Earl Navarro.'

'So you said,' Gillespie growled from behind the bar.

'Is he here?'

'I'm Navarro,' Earl said, and the kid turned and found himself looking into the barrel of Earl's .44.

'There's no need—'

'You think you're going to get out of here alive?' Earl asked.

The kid swallowed. 'I've got a message—'

'You said that already.'

The kid's eyes flicked around the saloon again.

'What's the message, son?' Gillespie said.

The kid looked at Gillespie and then at Earl Navarro. He swallowed once more. 'Mr Coleman's got your girl. He said—'

'She ain't my girl.'

'What?'

'She ain't my woman.'

'But Mr Coleman. . . .'

'Seems he was mistaken.' He stared at the kid. There was confusion in the kid's eyes. 'So . . . you think that alters things a little?'

Now the kid looked hardly more than a boy. 'I . . . I don't know.'

'Tell us the rest of what Mr Coleman said.'

'He said . . . he said he wants to strike a deal.'

'Uh-huh.'

'He wants you.'

'He wants me what?'

'You're to ride over to the ranch. He'll let your . . . the lady go and have you instead.'

'And when am I to give myself up this way?'

'You can come now.'

Earl smiled. 'That's kind of you.' Now he spun the cylinder on his Colt just to remind the kid who was in charge.

'Or anytime before midday tomorrow.'

'I see. And if I don't?'

'The lady. . . .'

'The lady what?'

'He'll kill her.'

There was the sound of another revolver cylinder being spun in the far corner of the bar. Somebody mumbled something. Someone else swore.

'It's a shame he picked someone who ain't my woman then, isn't it?'

'He said—'

'Well, he was wrong.'

'I'm just passing on the message.'

'Were you the one who killed our friend today?' Earl asked.

'I wasn't there.'

'How do we know?'

'Honest. I was—'

'What do you think's going to happen to you?'

'What?'

'I mean right now. Three of us have got guns on you already. Let me ask you again: you think you're going to get out of this saloon?'

'Mr Coleman said. . . .'

'Mr Coleman said that if anything happens to you Louisa will be killed anyway,' Earl said. 'Am I right?'

The kid nodded.

'It's a real shame, ain't it?' Earl said, easing back the hammer on his gun, the action sounding loud and clear in the heavy atmosphere.

'Please,' the kid said. His held his hands before him. They were shaking.

'How old are you, son?'

'Seventeen.'

'Mr Coleman's getting a kid to do his dirty work for him now, huh?'

The kid said nothing, but he shook his head. Earl didn't know if the kid was disagreeing with the statement or simply trying to refute the whole situation.

Now Earl eased the hammer back down on his gun and he saw the boy let out a breath. 'You tell Coleman that if he's harmed one hair on Louisa's head then I'll personally scalp him. You got that?'

The kid nodded.

'Go on, then,' Earl said. 'Git, before I change my mind.'

The kid didn't move and just for a moment Earl was impressed. A lot of boys would already have been running out the door.

'Well?' he asked.

'What shall I tell Mr Coleman?'

'Tell him what I just told you.'

'Will you be coming?'

'Let's leave him in suspense, shall we?'

This time the kid nodded, took one final look around the bar, and backed out.

Frank told the others that he'd see them in town. He left them riding towards the area where George Clancy had been shot and he cut to the south in a large circle, riding hard for half an hour, then easing up, then riding hard again. He came up on the Double C ranch from the southwest.

The war was something from another lifetime: looking at maps and calculating losses in thousands and timescales in days and weeks; figuring out the logistics of keeping 10,000 men fed and watered and supplied with ammunition; planning for casualties and prisoners, considering alternative strategies and retreat routes; dovetailing the small picture into the large picture; battling to keep up with the news on events elsewhere and readjusting one's plans accordingly; climbing to the top of rises to scour the countryside looking for the small advantages that nature might offer.

It was this last one that he was doing now, and in the process it brought back the memories of that other lifetime, the smoke and the noise, the blood and the dust, the stench, the missing friends and the dead strangers, the annihilated land, his country torn in two and still not mended, and his surviving it all, a winner. But everyone who had been there had lost something and most cared not to reflect on it, although in some places back East you had no choice – the reminders were in front of you every day, the blind, the deaf, the men with no faces, no arms, no legs. Out here it wasn't so bad. It was easier to leave your memories behind. But they came to him now as he stared down on Coleman's ranch, noting the way that he was constructing double-timbered fencing around much of the site, big gates in the middle of the fence though you could have ridden round the back and got in without any problem. There were cowboys down there wearing guns, there was a long bunk house and a large stable, other smaller buildings, two huge corrals, and the ranch house itself the biggest building Frank had seen in a long time. It looked more like some of the houses they'd come across in the South. As he looked out over the ranch, his military experience analysing the weaknesses in the defence and the best lines of attack, another part of his mind was thinking about his sister. He'd hardly had time to see her since arriving here. It felt like he'd been thrown right into the middle of a battle. In a way that was true. Bud was dead, George Clancy, whom he had only known for a matter of hours was dead, another guy from town was dead. Earl was injured. Such times should be over and done with by now. Did they go through so much hell for nothing?

But, by the time he rode back to town, he at least had the information he needed to make a plan. The only trouble was, in any war, soldiers on both sides were liable to die.

Late that night in Gillespie's, Earl said, 'No one does anything until Louisa is back safely in our hands.'

'You could be dead by then,' Bob Forrest said.

'No. If I've read Coleman right he'll be wanting to keep me alive, not kill me.'

'He's not likely to be cooking you a meal and breaking out his finest wine,' Sonny Roux said.

'I know that.'

'We'll be waiting,' Frank said. 'We'll be as quick as we can.'

'I know you will.

'I want to come, too.' The voice was that of a child. They all looked round. The boy stood in the doorway, his face lit by an oil lantern hanging just inside the bar. He had a rifle resting across his arms.

'We want all the men we can get,' Gillespie said. 'And it's very brave of you, son, but—'

'They killed my pa. You can't stop me coming.'

Earl looked across the room at the Clancy boy, his face fire orange and tear-stained, a look of determination across his mouth. Earl felt pride and sorrow mixed inside him. This was a good town. They didn't deserve what had happened to them. They hadn't asked for it. They hadn't done anything to bring it upon themselves and now some of them were homeless, one of theirs had been kidnapped, and three were dead. Maybe more would be dead come the morrow. But that hadn't stopped them turning up at Gillespie's in their dozens, all ready to ride into battle. They weren't soldiers: they were just barbers and storekeepers, lumber merchants and small-holders, and now a kid. Yet they'd taken all they could and they were ready to stand up for what was right. It was a fine feeling and yet it was a sad feeling. The war should have put an end to this. Anybody who had been there thought that it would. The war to end wars. And yet there was always something else, someone else, another reason to fight.

Earl stood up. His leg hurt and his body ached. He suddenly felt too old for this. Maybe this would be his last time. Then again, maybe it wouldn't be his choice. It hadn't been his choice this time, really. His past followed him around like a shadow and wherever he went folks seemed to expect something from him. He wondered if it would always be thus.

He walked across the saloon and crouched down in front of the boy. Pain from his leg sliced into his belly but he didn't let it show.

'Son, do you know how to shoot that?'

'I've killed rabbits.'

'See all these men here?'

'Yep.'

'Seems to me that it's most of the men in town. Now I know you want to ride with us on account of what happened to your pa, but we're going to need someone to stay behind in town and look after all the women.'

'Yeah but—'

'It's more important than riding out. The men we're after snuck up on our town once before, that's how they got Miss Louisa. There's going to be a few men here but we need all the help we can get. You think you can do that for me?'

The boy looked at Earl and Earl looked back. The kid was trying hard not to cry, but at the same time there was a determination and courage in his eyes that Earl wasn't sure was reflected in his own.

'I can do that,' the boy said.

'Good man. You be up at dawn tomorrow and Mr Gillespie here will give you your orders, OK?'

The boy nodded. 'OK.'

'Now go and sleep, son. Tomorrow's a big day.'

After the boy left, Earl limped back to the bar. 'One more for good luck,' he said. 'And then another.'

They rode out three hours before dawn, Frank alongside

Earl at the head of the line of riders. The moon illuminated them, most men riding in pairs, very few speaking,
unsure of what lay ahead and scared because they knew
that some of them mightn't make it back. Old Man
Gallagher watched them go. He'd stayed up with them all
night in Gillespie's, drinking, and listening to Frank
outline his plans. The newcomer had requested dynamite.
The general consensus was that there wasn't any in the
town, but then Ray Benson who ran the mercantile said he
might be able to help in that regard. He disappeared for
fifteen minutes and when he returned he placed a
wooden box on the table.

'Is that enough?' he asked.

Frank had told him it was perfect and Old Man
Gallagher had smiled to himself. Coleman was sure going
to have a surprise.

Now, riding towards the west with the night chill still
cutting through their clothes, Frank looked across at Earl
Navarro and said, 'Are you OK?'

'Yep.'

'You know you don't have to go in there first.' Frank
twisted round and looked back over the column. 'We've
got enough men, more'n twenty, to simply ride straight in
there.'

'You know we can't do that. We have to get Louisa out
first.'

'I know. I was just giving you the chance to—'

'It's OK. I'm easy with it.'

Frank nodded.

'We'll be as quick as we can.'

'I appreciate it.'

After that they rode across the plain in silence, each

thinking his own thoughts, Frank pondering on the finer points of besieging Coleman's ranch and Earl staring up at the stars wondering if he was going to be alive to see them – or Louisa – again. And though he tried not to think about it, he couldn't help but wonder what Coleman had planned for him when he walked through the man's gate and surrendered.

CHAPTER ELEVEN

Thomas Coleman sat in the darkness of his dining-room smoking a cigar and staring out at the night when he heard footsteps on the hall floor. The door opened and one of the Mexicans' heads peered round.

'Mr Coleman?' the Mexican asked hesitantly, then when he saw the burning cigar he opened the door wider and repeated the words. 'Mr Coleman. A man is coming.'

Coleman took another draw on his cigar. He let the air slip out of his lungs, closed his eyes and tilted his head back, letting the neck muscles stretch. It had been a long night. He hadn't known what to expect. Something would happen, he knew that, but he hadn't known exactly what.

'How far out is he?'

'He's here.'

'Here? Where?'

'Outside the gates. Just sitting there on his horse.'

'OK. How many of the boys are awake?'

'Just a few. Just the ones on your look-out. You want me to let the man in?'

'Let him stay where he is for a little while.'

'Are we going to let the girl go?'

Thomas Coleman looked out at the night again. Then

he turned back to the Mexican. 'No. No, I don't think we will.'

Earl Navarro waited before the large wooden gates in front of the Double C ranch house. He knew he had been seen; there had been movement and whispers, but so far nothing had happened. The gates weren't really a barrier, he could see between the timbers and he could have climbed over very easily – at least he could have done had his leg not felt as stiff and immobile as a board. Even more easily he could have ridden around. He knew that the fence didn't enclose anything. It was purely symbolic, or maybe a work in progress. Actually, the ranch was so huge and sprawling there seemed little point in fencing it in. Not out here, anyway, where there was unlikely ever to be any passing trouble. Earl smiled to himself. This morning excepting, he thought. Nevertheless, passing traffic or not, the place had been built to impress. The house was huge, the yard and the corrals covering almost as much land as some towns he had been in. Whatever Coleman was, it wasn't modest. Earl wondered what they were doing inside? Someone was probably waking up all of the men. If he'd read Coleman right then the man would be taking no chances whatsoever at losing him this time. And he would be licking his lips at the prospect of what was to come. On the other hand, if he'd read Coleman wrong then they might simply shoot him, a bullet out of the darkness just like the ones he'd fired himself, the thought still bringing with it a touch of self-loathing and guilt. His shoulders were tight with tension and his belly felt uneasy. Frank had told him that it was a crazy idea. 'You'll be setting yourself up as a target,' he'd said.

'Maybe,' Earl had said. 'But I think he's more cruel than that.'

'I hope you're right,' Frank had said, and then realizing the implications said, 'Well, it ain't good either way.'

Earl resisted the urge to look behind and around him. He knew dawn was breaking, the sky in the east lightening, making him even more of a target, and he knew that Frank and Bob and the others were out there somewhere, still a way back, but close, some of them circling, taking up the positions that Frank had chosen for them. Earl didn't want to give anything away so he sat still and stared at the unmoving gate.

After waiting long enough for dawn to have reached the edges of his forward facing vision there was more movement in the yard beyond the gates. As the gates swung open Earl saw several tall men with guns levelled at him, a couple more on horseback, a pair of Mexicans pulling the gate, plenty more cowboys around the edges of the yard including the boy they had sent to Gillespie's the night before, and in the middle a man with a beard, hooded eyes, a neck-tie, and a horsewhip. The cowboys on horseback immediately came through the gate and split left and right, taking up station behind Earl.

The man with the beard stepped forward. He had a cigar in the fingers of his left hand. It crossed Earl's mind that he could shoot the fellow – and a bunch of his men – before the man even realized that Earl hadn't come in peace. But he knew he couldn't shoot them all, and what would that mean as far as Louisa was concerned? Frank was unlikely to be close enough for any such changes in plan to be effective.

The man stared at Earl. Earl stared back. Neither

spoke. Eventually one of the tall cowboys said, 'You want to undo your belt and drop your guns on the floor?'

Earl ignored him and continued to stare at the bearded man.

Coleman took a long draw on his cigar. As the smoke escaped through his nostrils he said, 'I didn't think you'd come.'

'You going to let the lady go now?'

'In a moment.'

'Now's as good a time as any. I want to see her on a horse riding away.'

'You think you're in any position to make demands?'

'You don't strike me as a fool, Coleman.'

'Indeed I'm not. And, I must say, I never took you for a fool. Yet here you are. Now, you do as Wesley suggested and drop your guns.'

'Uh-huh.'

There was the sound of a rifle action being worked to his left, then another to his right.

'I'm sure you thought long and hard about how you were going to play this, Mr Navarro,' Coleman said. 'And I suspect you have one or two tricks up your sleeve. But the fact is right now you're surrounded and you make one wrong move and you're a dead man.'

'You too, Coleman. You too.'

'You'd happily shoot me as your last living act, would you?'

'Nothing would give me greater pleasure. Now, let the woman go.'

'Your guns, first.'

'We could stay here all day, Coleman.'

'No. *We* could stay here all day. You'll not be able to.'

'In which case I might get bored and shoot you. You might like to start by letting me see Louisa.'

Coleman nodded, then held up his hand and clicked his fingers. A few moments later one of his men came into sight holding Louisa by the upper arm. She had her hands tied behind her back. When she saw Earl with a dozen guns trained on him she cried out, 'No! You shouldn't have come.'

'As you can see, she's perfectly fine,' Coleman said.

'Now she's here you may as well saddle her up a horse,' Earl said, letting his eyes linger on Louisa's face for just a moment before forcing himself to look back at Coleman. Now wasn't the time for sentimentality.

'You know I could simply have you shot,' Coleman said. Earl could see how much he was savouring this. All his men were, too. They were grinning and laughing and spitting tobacco juice on the ground and generally enjoying the moment. It's foreplay to them, Earl thought. They have revenge on their minds for the killing I've done. They are relishing every moment.

'You won't shoot me,' Earl said. 'You have too many other plans for me.

Now Coleman smiled. 'Maybe so. Which makes it all the more surprising you're here. You must be more of a fool than I thought.'

And the thing is, Earl thought, maybe he's right. I've dealt him all the best cards in the deck and I've still bet everything I have on an unseen hand. At least all this talking would give Frank and the others time to get up as close as they could. He'd put his faith in the stranger and now had to endure whatever lay ahead for however long it took. And if the gamble failed? Well, for him it would be over *relatively* quickly. Only God knew what it would mean for the town. He suspected Coleman's revenge would not be satiated by one killing alone, no matter how long and painful that killing was.

'A saddled horse for Louisa,' Earl said.

Coleman clicked his fingers and now the man holding Louisa dragged her out of sight again.

'All this because of a one-legged farmer and his family,' Coleman said.

'No. All this because when a man takes everything that he wants time and time again sooner or later someone has to stand up to him.'

'You talk bravely for a fool, Mr Navarro. When you're . . . uh . . . no longer standing up to me, what then?'

'I suspect that my bravery will inspire others.'

'I see. A martyr.'

'History is full of them.'

'Indeed. And what do they all have in common?'

Earl smiled. 'They are remembered with affection. They are glorified and they continue to inspire even after they've gone.'

'They all died, Mr Navarro. They all died.'

Frank had eight of the men circling way back to come at the ranch from the west. Earlier, in the darkness outside Gillespie's, he'd told them to make as big a loop as they could and then edge up to the high ground and lie low waiting for his signal. 'You might want to have one or two men riding ahead – scouts,' he'd said, the words a suggestion, but the tone more of an order. 'That way, if Coleman's got some guards posted out there – and I didn't see any yesterday but that ain't to say he won't have any up there this morning – they might not be overly suspicious. You might have to kill them. Can you do that?'

'We can do that,' Josef Alvarez said. Other men murmured in agreement. George Clancy had been everybody's friend; Mannie Beauvais, too. And what had been done to the Laskies touched everyone.

'If you have to kill them it might be best to wait for my signal. Keep them talking until you hear me. And then. . . .'

'I can kill them quietly, if you like,' Josef said.

At the time Frank hadn't been able to see the man's eyes and hadn't wanted to offend him by somehow insinuating that his bravado might be misplaced. On the other hand, what was a man's pride compared to the success of the mission as a whole? Earl Navarro would be inside the ranch complex. God knew what Coleman would be doing to him. They didn't want a badly timed pistol shot ringing out across the plain as a warning, or indeed one of Coleman's men racing back down the hill to sound the alarm.

'It's not always as easy as you think,' Frank said. 'Not close up.'

Now Josef flicked a match into life with his thumbnail and in the flare Frank saw the man's narrow eyes and bearded face, his mouth set in determination.

'I can kill them quietly,' Josef repeated. 'I've done it before.' That raised a rumble of conversation from the other men.

Frank held up his hands and called for silence. He explained how he would leave some men – the older volunteers – back along the trail to cover their rear. The rest would edge as close as cover would allow, and as soon as Louisa Glanton was out of there they would split into two groups, one led by Bob Forrest and one by Frank, ready for an assault.

'What happens if he doesn't release Miss Louisa?' someone asked.

'Once Earl's in there we're not going to give it long. If Coleman doesn't release Louisa then we follow the plan exactly as we discussed earlier, only this time we have to get two of them out of there.'

'And the dynamite is the signal?'

'Yes,' Frank said. 'Depending on where they've got him I'm going to blow up his house. It's just to create confusion really, but as soon as we do that Bob and his men will come round on the south side. And Josef and the rest of you guys I want to come in on the back of the ranch.'

Back there it had seemed like a fine plan. It *was* a fine plan. A bit simplistic maybe, but then this wasn't a war and these guys – on either side – weren't soldiers. What would appear chaotic to the defenders would hopefully be logical and understandable to his men. He told them to watch who they were shooting at, especially when they were all coming from opposite directions and he told them it might be very frightening, terrifying even, but that's how it's meant to be. He told them those who were coming down from the foothills in the west were to hold station on the perimeter whilst his group and Bob's group went in and got Earl. He told them not to panic. And he told them that some of them might get shot.

Then he asked if any of them wanted to back out. They were all volunteers, storemen, card-players, farmers, smiths, Nathaniel the barber; but no sign of Garvey the sheriff. None of them chose to leave. But as they turned to head out of town a silence descended over them.

Now Frank lay on his belly in the dirt and watched, through Earl's telescope, the stand-off at the gates of the Double C.

Thomas Coleman was convinced that Earl Navarro had something up his sleeve. It was suicide to come here this way. And not a painless suicide either. Surely no man, not even a saint, would willingly give himself over for torture and death? Then again, Coleman thought, maybe I'm simply projecting my own character onto this man. Was it conceivable that someone really would give up everything for the sake of a woman? Coleman chewed on the end of his cigar, watched Navarro sat out there just beyond the gate, and spat on the ground. Horseshit, was what it was. Navarro had something up his sleeve. The guy wasn't a saint.

His men brought Louisa Glanton back into the yard. They'd put her on a pinto with a bad leg, though she didn't know that, and it wouldn't become apparent to her for about ten minutes. They could easily give her a twenty-minute start and still have her back here to watch the fun with Navarro.

But what about Navarro? Did he have hidden guns? Hidden men somewhere on the trail behind him? Probably both.

Coleman looked over at Navarro and smiled. He believed he was at least one step ahead of him. 'Your guns,' he said. 'Drop them now and ride in slowly. You can pass the lady at the gate.'

'She goes first.'

'I don't think so, Mr Navarro.'

The two men stared at each other. Coleman found it hard to maintain the smile, so he let his mouth straighten. 'The guns, Mr Navarro. I'll let Miss Glanton go as soon as your belt is on the floor. And the rifle in your scabbard, too.'

Still they stared at one another until eventually, with the sun a ball of fire behind him, Earl Navarro reached down and undid his belt and laces and held his guns out beside him.

Then he dropped them.

Frank wondered if Earl wanted to die. He watched his new friend drop his guns and he watched one of Coleman's cowboys slap Louisa's horse on the rump and he saw her ride out, pause beside Earl for a moment, her head shaking, his unmoving, and then he saw her ride on, Coleman's boys either side of Earl moving in closer now, rifles raised. He saw a muzzle flash from one of the guns and a moment later he heard the report. He saw Louisa look round. He saw Earl's horse crumple to the ground and then half a dozen of Coleman's men rush Earl, kicking and stamping, hauling him to his feet and dragging him into the Double C.

It was time to go.

But before he even dropped the telescope he saw Coleman's mounted men chasing after Louisa, gaining on her, rifles raised.

'Bastard,' he said, and prepared for battle.

CHAPTER TWELVE

When they shot his horse he hit the ground on his wounded leg. The pain wasn't as bad as he'd expected but it was enough to prevent him regaining his feet straight away. By the time he straightened his leg enough to put some weight on it they were on him, kicking him back down, feet coming at him from all directions. He curled into as small a ball as he could and wrapped his arms around his head. A toe connected with his spine, a heel ground into his ear, a boot split the stitches in his leg and another smashed between his hands and bloodied his mouth. One ear was ringing and the other was filled with the sound of his own laboured dirt-filled breathing, But then it was over and they were backing off, just two of them roughly tearing his jacket from him, checking his waistband for guns. They hauled him to his feet and through eyes that were already closing he saw Coleman standing in front of him, cigar in his mouth, a look of easy won victory in his eyes. Earl spat a mouthful of blood onto the ground between them.

'Still glad you came, Mr Navarro?'

Earl said nothing. All around him men were smiling and laughing and trying to catch their breath after the exertions of the kicking. Earl's early morning shadow stretched all the way to Coleman. Somewhere back to the east Earl heard a rifle shot. It sounded too close to be Frank. Surely he couldn't be here yet? But it would be soon – hopefully. Earl didn't want his shadow to get too much shorter before the Yankee came and saved him.

'I'll take your silence as a no. Or maybe as fear. Fear would be wise, Mr Navarro.'

The echo of the gunshot still reverberated in his mind.

'I trust you're a man of your word, Coleman,' Earl said, the words muffled in his swollen mouth, lubricated with blood from his broken lips.

'Absolutely,' Coleman said.

Earl held Coleman's stare and without conscious thought he found himself praying, not for his own salvation, but for just for a few seconds of freedom sometime before the end, just long enough to get his hands on the cattle baron.

'Tie his hands,' Coleman said. 'And bring him through to the yard.'

They tied his wrists together behind his back and took him around the side of the huge house and into the courtyard beyond. His wounded leg felt numb and the other felt bruised to twice its normal size. For every yard he managed to walk himself they dragged him two. As they hauled him along Coleman kept pace with him, talking constantly, smoking that big cigar, waving his hand in the air, explaining how he wasn't a bad man, it was just that the folks thereabouts didn't understand him.

'They don't have *vision* enough, Mr Navarro. They have no concept of *ambition*. They have no idea of what drives a man like me, Mr Navarro. Or, indeed, of the sacrifices that someone like me must make. They don't realize how much it hurts to chase after one's destiny the way I do.'

Earl did his best to ignore the man. On his right, a long building blocked his vision of the outside world, but across the yard to his left, he could see up into foothills of the great mountains. He tried to keep his look to just a swift glance, making it appear as if he was simply glaring at the cowboys keeping pace with him on that side, but up there on the foothills he believed he saw movement, tiny black dots coming closer. But then maybe it was just imagination – wishful thinking – or even false images created by the swellings that had half dosed his eyes, for wasn't the plan for the guys up there to stay hidden until Frank gave the signal to attack?

'The thing is, Mr Navarro,' Coleman was saying, 'once you're gone then I'm sure things will soon get back to the way they were. You've been somewhat of a ... *catalyst* in the town's rebellion. Without you it's just ... a yellow town.'

Now Earl could feel horses approaching from behind, the heavy thump of their hoofs on the hard ground. His neck and back hurt too much for him to twist round and try and see who it was.

'Of course, I could just shoot you. Have done with it, as it were. And believe me, if it were down to me – if all I was hoping to achieve was your ... *demise* – then that's exactly what I would do. In fact, I would have done so earlier when you were sitting on your horse, a broken man, outside my gates. You see, I'm not a cruel man. I'm really not.'

The horses came close behind now, slowing. A brief beacon of hope flared in Earl's foggy mind that it might be

Frank and the boys already. But as he worked a tooth loose with his tongue and spat it out onto Coleman's yard he forced himself to acknowledge that it wouldn't be them. Not yet. They had too far to ride to be here in seconds. It would be minutes. Long minutes.

'The thing is, just shooting you wouldn't have been enough, Mr Navarro. No. You see, there's the matter of Papa Davey, and Perry and Joe. And someone shot Cal, too. Was that you? I think maybe it was. Cal was a good man, Mr Navarro. They were *all* good men. Worst of all – for both of us – you shot Jared, one of my own sons. Shot him in the back from what I hear.' Coleman sighed. 'You understand, there's a certain amount of, uh, sufferance required to make up for all of that. You could say it's my duty. You do understand, I hope.'

Earl said nothing. Ahead of him, just in front of a wall he could see a pole set vertically into the ground with a small cross beam way above head height. It looked like a distorted crucifix. Rope hung from the cross beam. The ground around the base of the pole was stained brown.

'But there's more, I'm afraid, Mr Navarro. I also have to make an example of you. Something to illustrate to the townsfolk that they really oughtn't to mess with me. So suffering it is. And, of course, I need someone to be able to report on your punishment. Hence. . . .'

Now Coleman took a step away from Earl and pointed back. The two men dragging Earl turned him.

'I've not gone back on my word,' Coleman said. 'I shall release the lady. But only once she's been witness to your punishment.'

Louisa was there, a deep cut and a bruise on the left side of her beautiful face. Her clothes were dirty and her hands tied. She'd been thrown over the front of one of Coleman's men's horses like a sack of oats and now he dropped her to the ground. She was swearing, cursing and spitting at Coleman, trying to get to him, his boys laughing and pushing her back like a cruel game they might play with a coyote pup. Then she tripped and she knelt there on her knees, tears spilling silently down her face and her eyes met his.

'The pole,' Coleman said. 'Take him to the pole.'

After Coleman's men had turned back into the ranch, dragging Earl with them, and as soon as the two riders had shot Louisa Glanton's horse from beneath her, knocked her down once or twice to, Frank guessed, try and crush the spirit from her, and then hauled her back to the Double C, Frank and Bob both started to advance on the ranch. Bob took his men in a loop to come up from the south, Frank was headed straight for the gate and the house beyond it. The undulations of the land covered the horse-borne men much of the way. Once the cover ran out, Frank stopped the advance and dismounted. He stuffed several sticks of dynamite into his shirt, told the men that when they heard the explosions to ride like devils down into the Double C, not to kill one another, to look out for Earl and Louisa, but to kill anyone else.

Then he set off in a crouched run, darting from one stunted plant to the next, from a hole in the ground to a pile of rocks, to a tuft of coarse prairie grass, all the time getting closer and closer to Coleman's fence. The sun was still low behind him but he was sweating like it was midday; his breathing was fast and harsh and within a hundred yards he had a stitch in his side. He wasn't used to running. Nevertheless, the thought that Earl Navarro was completely in the hands of Coleman made the heavy breathing and the pain seem like nothing more than horsefly bites. He knew only too well from the war the terrible things that one man could do to another and he knew that every second he left Earl in that man's hands was a second too long.

As he weaved his way forward he wondered if Coleman had guards looking out over the approaches to the ranch. He ought to have. But there again, how many men would be concentrating on the land outside when inside their sworn enemy was being tortured? At least in this regard Earl's fate was a bonus, albeit not one Frank would have chosen for his new friend.

He twisted his foot in a hole as he ran and the pain arced up his leg but he didn't pause or cry out. Things were moving now and he had to keep going.

Closer and closer he went to the fence, expecting any moment for someone to cry out and then to hear the sound of a rifle shot and maybe feel the punch of a bullet or, if he was lucky, see the dirt kick up in front of him.

But neither the cry nor the gunshot came and, with his heart feeling like it was about to beat its way free of his chest and his face streaming with sweat, he finally slid up against the fence, too close now to be seen by guards even if they were there.

He took a moment to compose himself. He could hear voices and laughter from the yard beyond the house, horses snorting. He'd have liked to take a few men out with the initial blast but he didn't want to risk hurting Louisa or Earl. Earl had reckoned that Coleman had twenty-five men. A few killed right away would even the odds nicely. Still, maybe after the first blast he'd get a few seconds of confusion in which he could more carefully direct the second stick of dynamite. He opened up his shirt, pulled out three sticks, and dug a half-dozen lucifers from his pocket.

What was the best plan? Roll a stick under the house? Throw another up on the roof? Maybe come in firing through the smoke? Bob Forrest would hit the south side within seconds of the explosions. Frank's own group would catch up moments later and, just as Coleman figured he had the shape of the attackers sorted in his mind, Josef's band would attack from the west, too. Once Frank knew where Earl and Louisa were he'd throw the rest of the dynamite about, too.

He stuffed one of the sticks in the dirt at the base of the fence, flicked the match into life with his thumbnail and lit the fuse.

Then he lit two more and lobbed them gently over the fence and watched them roll under Coleman's porch.

As he was about to run back along the fence for cover he heard Louisa scream 'No!' and he heard a sob catch in her throat. Then came a mighty grunt of pain from Earl Navarro. He knew such a noise couldn't have come from anyone but a man determined not to scream but needing to let out his agonies somehow. Frank had rarely seen men able to contain their pain that way, but once or twice he'd seen rebel prisoners who'd clenched their teeth and let the scream come from their throats rather than their lungs. The first few times, anyway. Once they'd been weakened the screams soon came. If only such men had realized that half the time it was the screams that their torturers wanted to hear and fighting the pain only made things worse. Nevertheless, he understood such men and had always been quietly impressed by their bravery.

The sound of Earl's agonies had stopped him in his tracks. Now he dived for cover.

For a moment there was no additional pain. Earl figured they were just tying him to the post, that the loops hanging down from the cross-beam were for tying men's hands up there and letting them hang. He guessed they were going to beat him, maybe whip him, cut him, maybe even brand him. But for the moment it was nothing he couldn't bear.

Then two of Coleman's men behind him hauled down on a piece of rope and suddenly Earl's arms were wrenched upwards, against the joints feeling like they were going to pop out from their sockets. His reaction was to scream – he'd never felt such pain in all his life. Almost his entire weight was held by his twisted arms – but he managed to stifle the scream and instead let out a grunt. He was on tiptoes, trying as hard as he could to keep his weight on his toes. The men behind him laughed and wrapped the rope around something to keep it tight.

Tears rolled down Earl's face. He was tilted downwards by the pain and by his own weight, seeing only the dirt and the boots of his tormentors. He tried to raise his head but the pain was incredible, even the beating of his heart was agony. Louisa was crying and begging them to show him mercy. His breathing was ragged and harsh and loud. The flow of blood sounded like rushing water in his ears.

'Hurts, don't it?' someone said.

'You scream if you want to,' someone said. 'You're going to sooner or later, anyways.'

'One more inch and that feeling you got now will seem like the best feeling you ever had,' another said.

'We had a fellow last two hours once afore he blacked out,' another cowboy said. 'Well, he was an Indian, so maybe that don't count.'

'Yeah, but most of 'em go out straight away. We throw water over 'em, Navarro. Wake 'em up, like. Generally we don't shoot them until they're really begging for it.'

Louisa was still weeping. Now Earl managed to straighten his head. Coleman was smoking his cigar impassively. Once again they stared at each other. Earl hadn't the strength to speak. Coleman said, 'And you will beg, Mr Navarro. What they say is correct. When we haul you up so your toes are no longer on the ground you'll scarcely believe the pain.'

Earl shook his head. There seemed to be no reason for this. Killing a man he could understand. Torturing a man for information he could understand, But this. . . .

'I'm in a charitable mood, Mr Navarro. I've no idea why. Maybe we should move things on. What do you say?'

Earl coughed and blood stained the dirt in front of him.

'Another couple of inches, boys,' Coleman said. 'I really hate to do it. Really, I do.'

When they hauled him off the ground Earl thought that both his shoulders had been dislocated. Coleman and his cowboys had not only been right, if anything they had underplayed the pain. This time he had no choice but to scream. Yet as he opened his mouth and screwed his eyes shut it seemed that the whole world screamed with him. There was a mighty explosion and sound-waves and air-pressure hit him as solidly as any punch ever had. The blast swung him out on the rope like a pendulum and the pain increased but then there was another blast and now bricks and pieces of wood were flying through the air and smoke darkened the sky and clogged the lungs. A third blast and someone else was screaming, too. Other people were shouting. Somebody fired a gun. He cried out to Louisa but his voice was lost in the echo of the blast and then the pain came again and he was unable to say a word, unable to do anything but swing there, straining with every ounce of strength he had left to try and hold himself up.

And somewhere in the midst of the chaos he could still hear Coleman. The man was coughing and cursing, but his words came through the ringing remnants of the explosion loud and clear.

'Kill Navarro,' he cried. 'Kill Navarro.'

The moment the blast of dynamite went off Bob Forrest swallowed the bile that was threatening to make his fear visible, dug his spurs into his horse's flanks, let out a yell, and galloped out of the cover and across the last fifty yards towards the Double C ranch. Alongside him five other men did the same. The ground shook beneath the horses and dust rose up behind them. In seconds they were at the far end of the chest-high double-log fence. Bob's horse cleared it as if it didn't exist, landed in the yard where, despite the wind of the gallop and the blood and fear racing through his veins, he could already hear men screaming and yelling. Other men jumped the fence too, some simply rode around it. He led his small cavalry unit behind one corral and into the yard behind the big house and there they found smoke and chaos and a huge crowd of cowboys all firing into the smoke billowing from one corner of the house. There hardly seemed time to be scared, yet even as adrenalin rushed through his veins and his eyes fought to take in everything, he found his belly tying itself in knots and his throat dry. It would have been easy, tempting even, to give in to the fear, but instead he reined his horse to a skidding halt, pulled out his revolver and aimed at the crowd, only remembering at the last moment what Frank had said about watching who you were shooting at, especially with the townsfolk coming from three directions. In that brief moment of hesitation Bob saw several of the cowboys look round and cry out, he saw Louisa Glanton wrestling with a cowboy, he saw Earl hanging from a pole appearing to be unconscious, and then he saw something arc across the air from behind the house and wall and land on the roof of the long bunkhouse behind the crowd.

A bullet whistled through the air. Bob Forrest had no idea of how close it was. He aimed away from Louisa and Earl but into the crowd of cowboys and fired again and again. The men beside him were doing the same. 'Watch out for Louisa and Earl!' he cried.

Several of the cowboys they were shooting at went down. Something struck his horse in the chest hard enough for him to feel the shock and the next moment he was on the floor, still aiming, still firing until the Colt clicked onto empty chambers. Somebody screamed out beside him and wetness splattered his face.

Then the bunkhouse roof exploded, showering them all with dirt and wood and dust. A piece of twisted metal embedded itself in the ground about a foot in front of him. Somebody was moaning behind him. Ahead of him a cowboy dropped to the floor, his hat rolling away to reveal no head, just bloody shoulders.

Lying behind his horse, Bob Forrest tried to reload his pistol. But his hands were trembling so much that he dropped bullet after bullet before getting six in place and starting shooting again. Most of the cowboys ahead of him had split left and right seeking out cover now, some behind water barrels, some heading for other buildings. His own men were stuck out in the open.

'Find some cover!' he called, looking around seeing just the narrow poles of the corral fences, a buggy and some more dead horses for cover. Someone lay motionless beside him. There wasn't time to look closely to figure out who it was. The men started wheeling their horses, and retreating backwards.

In that moment Bob realized that the element of surprise was over and that Earl still hung from the pole and Louisa was now firmly in the grasp of the cowboy she had been fighting with.

Josef Alvarez saw the explosion a moment before he heard it. By then he was already leading his seven men in a race down the slopes to the ranch below. It was too far away. They could hear shooting, see the flashes of gunfire and the smoke and dust rising over the buildings. They saw Bob Forrest's men come rushing in, disappear from view behind some of the out-buildings and then reappear just a few moments later. They saw one of the townsfolk shot out of his saddle. Someone cursed and another whispered *Dear God*. By the time yet another explosion ripped through one of the buildings they were close enough to feel the air pressure and hear someone screaming after-wards.

There were men hiding in the new rubble of the bunk house firing back towards Bob Forrest's men. There'd been no guards back up in the foothills and Josef had been severely disappointed, although his disappointment was balanced by some of the other men's relief. Still, if they could get down there fast enough there would be an opportunity to avenge the deaths of his friends in town. The cowboys down there deserved everything they were about to get.

Josef and his riders were almost on top of the broken bunk house before the Double C men cowering inside realized they were there, the explosions and gunshots no doubt dulling their senses. As the defenders turned, Josef's men were upon them, firing at point-blank range, smashing with rifle butts those who were in the open crouching behind the remains of the rear wall, riding round the bunk house in two directions pouring gunfire into the building. Josef himself rode directly into the middle of the yard. He'd seen death before, massacres even, and this was the same. It was everything the Double C deserved.

Louisa screamed and jumped on the back of a man who was aiming his gun at Earl. His bullet went wide and thudded into the bunk-house wall. She had her fingers on his face, scratching for his eyes. She found something soft and he screamed and started bucking like an unbroken mustang. He elbowed her and threw her over his hip and onto the ground. She landed on her back and pain jarred up her spine and into her neck but she rolled to her left just as he aimed a savage kick at her. There was blood on his face. Now came another huge explosion and the man she'd been grappling with fell down. There were men on horseback coming around the far side of the house, guns blazing, more coming round the near corner. Everything was crazy and confused, smoke and dust filled the air, men were yelling instructions and advice to one another and some of them were screaming and moaning and cursing, horses were shrieking; the ground trembled as another explosion went off and debris whistled through the air. Part of her wanted to dive flat on the earth. Part of her wanted to run. But she could do neither. She had to get to Earl. He was helpless, suspended like an animal carcass, on the wooden pole.

She took one step towards him and then felt herself being swept off her feet and carried away towards the main house.

No bullet came. For a moment it would have been welcome, the pain was so bad. The agony such that it had been almost impossible to put coherent thoughts together. But now that he realized rescue might be just seconds away he somehow found the strength to hold on. It was impossible to do anything but hang there and try and bear the weight, try and use whatever muscles he could to last just a moment longer, then a moment more. One of the blasts must have loosened the rope a little for he could just get his toes on the ground again. The pain was still terrible but at least some of the weight was taken from his shoulders. He was aware of the second and third explosions, maybe even a fourth, of the arrival of some of the men on horses, and of an increase in gunfire and screaming, then of the gunfire becoming slightly less intense. He could hear the ground shaking as more men on horseback arrived. There was more shooting. More screaming. At one point he managed to raise his head and he saw Louisa being carried away from him. Whoever had her – and in the brief moment he was able to look, he thought it might have been Coleman himself – was heading for the main house. That was all he saw before the pain in his neck became too great and he had to lower his head.

Time passed. He had no idea whether it was seconds or minutes. He knew he'd lost consciousness at one point. It was a voice that brought him back.

'Hold on, buddy,' Frank said.

Frank had burst around the corner of the house into the mayhem created by the noise and smoke of the explosions. He'd shot two men before having to retreat temporarily, but by then he'd seen enough. He knew where Earl was; he knew where Louisa was. He lit another stick of dynamite and threw it onto the roof of a building behind everyone. Then he'd ducked backwards and gone back outside the yard, sprinting up the far side of the fence just as the dynamite exploded. More of his men were arriving now – Bob's group, too. He could see Josef's band streaming down from the hills. He clambered over the fence at a point where he hoped he wasn't expected, saw Louisa being carried towards the main house and took a bead on the man carrying her but through the smoke it wasn't a safe shot. He swore and watched her dragged inside. There were a dozen or more dead men on the ground around him, more over where Bob's group had joined the attack. He swore again. Now there was gunfire coming from within the main house. But Josef's men were at the perimeter keeping most of the other Double C cowboys busy.

He reached Earl.

'Hold on, buddy,' he said, pulling out his knife, cutting his friend loose, catching him as he fell, and immediately dragging him backwards to the shelter of the ruined bunk house.

'Louisa,' Earl said.

'We'll get her back,' Frank said, but then he felt something punch him in the back and he stumbled forward, a wetness flowing down the inside of his shirt.

Coleman threw Louisa onto the floor, turned and slammed the door. Immediately there was a hammering on the heavy wood, the handle turned, and several of his boys pushed their way in.

'Who's still out there?' Coleman asked.

One of the boys shook his head.

'What does that mean?' Coleman growled.

'They're all dead,' another cowboy said. He had blood soaking through his shirt at the shoulder. 'Or as good as.'

Coleman turned and looked at Louisa. She glared up at him and for a moment Coleman had an urge to draw his gun and shoot her. Behind the woman two of his Mexicans, a man and a girl, cowered on the stairs. The air was filled with smoke and dust and sunlight from the windows painted golden lines across the room. At the top of the stairs the sky could clearly be seen through a huge hole in the roof. The blast had knocked paintings off the walls and a mirror lay shattered on the hall floor.

Then there was silence.

'You've lost,' Louisa said. 'Whatever happens to me, whatever you do to me, you've lost.'

Coleman shook his head. He looked at the men around, just half a dozen of them had made it into the house. Wesley was there. But where was Lewis? Jack was there, too. Andreas, Shelby, Flynn and Jackson. That was it. The Mexicans didn't count. He heard someone shouting outside. The words were unintelligible beneath the whistling in his ears. It was almost incomprehensible. Everything had just gone crazy. How could it happen? The townsfolk had never lifted a finger before. Literally. Not a single finger. Garvey was in his pocket and the rest of them were simply happy that he wasn't bothering them. If he merely coughed most of them wet themselves in fear. So how could it happen? How could a yellow town suddenly rise up against him this way?

Someone was talking to him. He ignored them. He had a picture in his head: Earl Navarro. He'd had the man right where he wanted. For a few seconds back there he was master of all the world. If he could beat a man like Navarrao – and he had beaten him – then no one would ever stand up to him. Navarro had been hanging from the pole, from the *cross*, screaming in agony. That had been real. There should've been no one else with any courage out there. Sure, there'd been that shoot-out yesterday, but there was no doubting who was behind that. With Earl hanging it should have all been over.

Now he looked up and realized everyone was staring at him.

'What are we going to do?' Andreas asked.

'Did anyone shoot him?' Coleman asked. 'Navarro. Did anyone shoot him?'

They all shook their heads and Coleman found himself trembling, feeling the pressure rising inside his veins.

'You've lost,' Louisa said, still lying on the floor. 'They'll be coming through that door any moment.'

Coleman looked down at her.

No. He hadn't lost. He'd lost some men, that was all. Maybe another son. And someone would pay for that. But it was a hard world. He'd survived the Indian wars. He'd thrived in the War Between the States, selling cattle to both sides. He'd built up his business and lost it and built it up again. He'd had family killed on him before. But he hadn't ever *lost*. If he could just get down south he could raise an army big enough to burn down every single building in a hundred-mile radius. He could pick men who would relish the chance to cut through the tendons of all the menfolk in town and watch them slither like snakes while the women screamed and were driven away like cattle to some distant market. He could do all that and more, rebuild the ranch – make it bigger and even more impressive – and he could do it with just the loose change he had hanging around back in Texas. He could – and would – rule this part of the world.

Lost?

No, this was merely a opening skirmish in a war that would see every single one of them pay more dearly than they could ever imagine.

They all saw the change come over his face. Louisa was about to say something else but the words fell silently from her lips.

'It's going to be OK, ain't it?' Andreas said.

Coleman nodded.

'So long as we've got her, we can't lose.'

*

'Frank,' Earl said. 'Frank!'

The Yankee's eyes were closed. A dribble of blood ran from his mouth. Outside, men were moaning, one was screaming, another was cursing and another still was praying. Josef was calling out orders but Earl's ears felt full of cloth and he couldn't make out the words. He could feel rather than hear the sound of horses and men walking. Smoke brought tears to his eyes and he could smell gunpowder and blood and vomit.

'Frank,' he said again.

And then Louisa's scream cut across everything, the sound of it bringing back memories of his own recent agonies and with them the knowledge that Coleman was capable of any cruelty. Absolutely anything.

As the scream faded into choked sobs Coleman's voice came across the yard loud and clear.

'Do you want to make a deal, Navarro? Or do you want to sit there and listen to her die?'

CHAPTER THIRTEEN

All the men had to leave, Coleman said. Every single one of them. Afterwards Navarro was to stand in the middle of the yard.

'What about Louisa?' someone called. Earl thought it was Bob Forrest but couldn't be sure.

'She'll be fine so long as you do as I've asked.'

'You told us that once before.'

Earl went to say something but someone squeezed his arm. He looked down. Frank's eyes were open. The Yankee shook his head.

'I'm a man of my word,' Coleman called. 'I told you I'd release her and I would have done. It's not my fault you defaulted on the deal.'

'We'll track you down, Coleman,' someone else said. 'This isn't over by a long stretch.'

'Is it a deal? Do you want to hear her scream again? Help you make up your mind.'

'We'll chase you wherever you go.'

'There's no need. I'll be coming back.'

Now Bob Forrest was looking down at Earl. Bob's face was covered in dirt and blood. 'We should kill that sonofabitch,' he said. 'They shot Gage and Woody too.'

Earl's shoulders felt as if two hot knives had been slid into them. His body was a mess of bruises and swellings and his shot leg was bleeding.

'Tell him Earl's wounded,' Frank whispered, struggling to catch his breath. 'Tell him he can't walk to the middle of the yard.'

'Is it a deal?' Coleman called out.

'Earl's injured,' Bob Forrest said. 'Let me put him on a horse with the other men and *I'll* stand in the yard.'

'Who'm I talking to?' Coleman said.

'Bob Forrest.'

'I don't believe you, Forrest.'

'I think he's dying.'

'Tell him to crawl to the middle of the yard.'

'He took a shot in the belly. He can't crawl.'

'And you want to put him on a horse?' Coleman laughed. 'Some buddy you are.'

'He doesn't want to die here.'

'He's got no choice, Forrest. But you – and the others – you have. You can go now.'

'And if we don't?'

'You hear the girl die. Then we'll carry on the fight and maybe you boys will die too. Some of you will for sure.'

Bob looked back at Earl. Frank was whispering to him. Now Frank said to Bob, 'Tell him it's a deal. Get the boys rounded up but take your time leaving.'

'What about you?'

'We'll catch you up,' Earl said.

'Neither of you are in any fit state—'

'I'm waiting,' Coleman said.

'It's a deal,' Bob Forrest said quietly. 'But Earl can't move. You'll have to come and get him.'

148

Suddenly Louisa screamed again. The sound sent a shiver up Earl's spine.

'Sorry,' Coleman said. 'I just wanted to remind you boys of what's at stake if you were maybe thinking of playing a trick on me.'

'No tricks,' Bob Forrest said, looking at the bloodied stick of dynamite that Frank had pulled from inside his shirt and was handing to Earl.

Coleman watched them go. He wasn't going to get caught out a second time. His remaining boys monitored the exodus along the barrels of their rifles. They could have picked the men off one by one, but there was more of them – many more – than he'd anticipated. If they started firing again then almost everyone on both sides would die. There would be plenty of time to return and settle this score.

As the dust settled behind the departing townsfolk, their heads hanging in defeat and grief, Coleman walked across the room and looked out across his yard.

'Anything moving out there?' he asked Wesley, who'd been stationed at the window.

'Nope. Not now. They took their dead and they've gone like the yellow curs they are.'

There were still bodies on the ground outside – horses and men. The dirt was dark with blood and the ruins of his bunkhouse still smouldered.

'He's in there?'

'Yep. See his feet. Every now and again he twitches in pain.'

'You want to go and get him?'

'Nothing I'd rather do.'

'Go round the back. Sneak up on him. He's bound to

have a gun.'

Wesley nodded. 'It ain't over, is it?'

Coleman smiled coldly. 'The fun's just beginning.'

Frank believed he was dying. He'd seen enough gut-shot men before to know that it wasn't something you recovered from. It seemed incredulous that he could have survived that whole war and all the years since only to catch a bullet out here in the Godforsaken middle of nowhere.

He pushed his legs into the hard dirt trying to ease himself into a more comfortable position and trying to get where he could see the house a little better. Strangely the pain was not too bad now. He wondered if feelings starting to fade was the beginning of it? The beginning of the end.

But there was still one more job to do yet. He still had to give Earl a little time and space.

He waited as long as he felt was right then he yelled out, 'Where's the girl, Coleman?' His voice was already husky from the smoke and blood and he didn't have to add too much of a southern accent to sound just like Earl. 'Let me see her, please.'

For a moment nothing happened, then against one of the windows he saw a shape, a head, shoulders, reflections of the sky obscuring her, but Coleman wouldn't know that. He thought he heard her sob.

'Take a good look,' Coleman said. 'I hope she was worth it.'

'Louisa!' Frank cried.

Then from behind him he heard the action of a gun being worked and someone said, 'Hell, you ain't Earl Navarro.'

*

150

It seemed to Earl Navarro that the plan could never have worked. There had been too many unknowns, too many variables, too many things left to chance. Coleman could have shot him as he'd sat outside the gates on his horse. His guards could have picked off Frank before he'd set off the first blast that had signalled their attack. The men from town could have frozen – no one would have blamed them. Lordy, Frank had even had that dynamite cradled in his shirt. A bullet might have missed him and hit the explosives. They could all have been killed. There were any number of things could have happened. He thought back to Frank jesting with him and saying that no wonder the Yankees had won the war. It seemed to him now that it was a wonder anyone ever won a war. And with the thought came the revelation that war was simply down to which side could sustain the most casualties and still go on fighting. It wasn't about tactics: it was about slaughter.

Another thought came to him, especially pertinent considering what he was about to do – the explosions could have sent wood and nails and stones flying into Louisa and killed the very person they'd come to save.

He strained to listen out for Frank's call and when it came, and along with it Coleman's mocking reply and Louisa's sobbing he mentally placed her on the far side of the huge house. He lit the final stick of dynamite, placed it against the doorframe on the front of the house and pulled a wooden bench over the dynamite to help direct the blast inwards.

Then he took several steps along the porch, crouched down and prayed.

'We've been tricked!' Wesley cried, and Frank shot him in

151

the throat. The sound of the shot echoed across the otherwise still morning.

'Wesley,' someone called. 'Wesley, what's going on?'

And then, with timing that brought a smile to Frank's pale lips, there came a huge explosion from the far side of the house, and a few seconds later a rattle of gunshots, maybe a whole dozen.

After that there was silence again.

Through some strange combination of frame structure and physics the door to Coleman's mansion came flying outwards, yet most of the surrounding timber went inwards filling the hallway and the rooms beyond with more smoke and dust and splinters.

Earl Navarro followed the blast in, limping heavily but not noticing any pain. He came out of the smoke and dust with a borrowed gun in each hand. A shaft of light from the broken roof crossed the room and illuminated Louisa crouching by the window on the far side of the room, her hands tied behind her back, her red dress torn and blood on her shoulders.

It was the only orientation Earl Navarro needed.

He shot one man who was standing just beyond Louisa with a rifle in his hand then pumped several bullets into another who was fumbling to pull a revolver from his holster. Now someone at one of the windows across the room reacted and pulled a gun but Earl took a step forwards and shot him too, the man firing as he died but his bullet burying itself harmlessly in the roof. He heard footsteps behind him and he turned through ninety degrees and saw another man coming across the hallway outside. Both of Earl's guns blazed and the man fell.

He was aware that Louisa was staring up at him, her eyes wide with fear. He didn't know what she was thinking of him at that precise moment. It didn't matter to him, not then, not in the midst of the slaughter. He was what he was, and for a moment it wasn't even Louisa cowering there. It was Jessica kneeling over the young boy whom the Yankees had shot, terror in her eyes, a plea for mercy on her lips. All his life he'd wanted to avenge her and now it seemed that he had been given the chance.

But suddenly Louisa was back, now her eyes widening.

'Behind you,' she said.

He turned and there was a cowboy shielding himself with a small Mexican lady, one arm around her neck stifling her scream and almost lifting her off the ground, the other hand pointing a gun at him, pulling the trigger, the weight of the housekeeper making his aim wayward.

Earl Navarro raised his right arm and shot the man clean in the forehead, the bullet missing the woman by just three inches. As the man fell to the ground the house-keeper started screaming. Louisa scrabbled across the floor towards her.

Coleman stood in the middle of the room, his beard and his skin white with plaster dust and fear, defeat in his eyes.

'Your boys should have attended lessons with Bean,' Earl said.

'What?'

'They were too slow. They hesitated,' Earl Navarro said. And shot Thomas Coleman, who never had a gun, three times.

CHAPTER FOURTEEN

The first chill of autumn was in the air when Louisa Glanton paused outside Nathaniel's barbershop and looked down the street, beyond the town limits, at the mountains that rose up against the sky. Old Man Gallagher took his pipe from his mouth and made ready to speak, then thought better of it and carried on smoking. It was a shame to see such a pretty woman with that sad look always in her eyes. Most days she'd find a moment to come down here and stare out at the world. It was getting more and more difficult for Gallagher to know what to say to her.

Now she looked at him and smiled. 'How's Nathaniel?' she asked.

'He's doing fine, Miss Glanton. Walks a little slower but says it was a small price to pay.'

She looked back up at the mountains. 'You think he'll ever come back, Mr Gallagher?'

'Earl Navarro?'

'Yes.'

'He told you he would, didn't he?'

'Yes.'

'He always struck me as being a man of his word.'

'Maybe he was just trying to make it easier for me.'

'I don't see how telling you he would come back if he never intended to makes it easier, Miss Glanton.'

'No, I suppose not.'

'I still can't figure out why he went like that, in the middle of the night, I mean. Him being a hero and all.'

When Louisa looked at him it became even harder to figure out. The sadness in her eyes and the softness of her smile only served to make her even more attractive. If he'd had a woman like Louisa waiting on him he wouldn't be riding around some distant mountain trying to lay personal ghosts to rest. You could just as easy figure that stuff out whilst lying in the arms of a good woman.

'I think he felt guilty,' she said. 'A lot of men died. . . .'

'Most of 'em bad, too,' Gallagher said. 'Seems to me that God was looking down on our boys that day, save for Woody and Gage, of course. May their souls rest in peace.'

'He felt guilty about all of them,' Louisa said. 'He told me that he couldn't help what he was. He said if he couldn't live with what he was, how could he expect anyone else to?'

'What did you say?'

'It was hard.' Now Gallagher saw tears start to form in her eyes. 'What I saw him do. . . .'

Gallagher went to say something but again couldn't think of the right words.

'Maybe I scared him off. Maybe if I'd have been stronger. The thing is . . . I understand it more now. I just needed time.'

'Aye, and that's all he needed too, Miss Glanton.'

She ran the back of her hand across her eyes.

155

'I hope so,' she said. 'I surely do.'

Frank Murray was cutting a log to length for his and Jeannie's new corral when he sensed movement behind him. He let the log down slowly and turned gingerly, the muscles in his shoulder and chest still apt to complain now and then.

There was no one there.

He swore and bent down to pick up the log again. At first the pain had been good. For months he'd almost welcomed it. It had been proof that he was still alive. He'd woken in a bed in Coleman's house with a Mexican woman holding a cup of water to his lips. Even then he thought he was going to die, but somehow he hadn't. The best he could figure it the bullet had gone in, clipped his shoulder blade and twisted and turned inside him before popping out without touching anything crucial. He'd lost a lot of blood but somehow – a miracle maybe, and on reflection that day had seemed full of miracles – he'd survived. It had taken four months to recover even this much but every day still felt like a bonus. Nevertheless, he was now starting to get a little tired of the pain.

He lifted the log back into position and then he heard movement again. 'Chris'sakes!' he said, and turned round.

'I just can't figure out how you guys won the war,' Earl Navarro said. 'I mean, not only did you get yourself shot when no one else could even *buy* a bullet, but here I am sneaking up on you like I was a ghost.'

'Earl!' Frank dropped the log, a huge grinning stretching across his face. 'Earl Navarro as I live and breathe.'

'You're looking well, Frank.'

'You too. Never figured on seeing you again.'

'I told you I'd be back.'

'I figured it was just talk.'

'Where's the family?'

'They're in town. They ain't going to believe this. Are you here to stay?'

Earl looked towards the west. 'I was here to stay last time. Felt like I brought too much trouble to everyone.'

'I ain't even going to bother answering that. So what you been doing, Earl?'

'Riding around. Trying to lose all that trouble that was following me.'

'Did you succeed?'

'I guess I'll never know. But I feel . . . easier with it all now.'

'You know she asks about you every time I get into town.'

'Louisa?'

'Yep.'

'She saw what I did to Coleman and his men. I can't imagine she asks after me with much affection.'

'If you believe that then why are you back?'

Earl looked out in the general direction of the town again. Then he said, 'So you're a farmer now?'

'A man can change, Earl.'

'We are what we are. We do what we do.'

'There's not the conviction in those words that there was the first time round, Earl.'

Earl smiled.

'So what are you going to do, my friend?' Frank said.

'About what?'

'About the lady who asks after you every day?'

Earl's fingers tightened on the horse's reins. 'I guess I'll be riding on into town now, Frank.'

'You know that they're looking for a new sheriff?'

'Really?'

'Garvey lit out a few months back.'

'So you're trying to fix me up with a job as well as a woman, are you?'

Frank smiled. 'Just trying to make the place look appealing.'

'Storm coming,' Earl said, glancing at the sky over Frank's shoulder.

Frank looked round. The sky was clear blue all the way to the mountains. When he turned back Earl was already ten yards away, riding in the direction of town, one hand raised. It was either a greeting or a farewell.

Frank figured on the former.